Discovery of an Eagle

Grace Mattioli

Library of Congress Cataloging-in-Publication Data
Mattioli, Grace, 1965-
Discovery of an Eagle/ Grace Mattioli.
p. cm.

1.Road Fiction 2.Families-Fiction 3.Italian Americans-Fiction 4.United States-Fiction 5.Spiritual Fiction

I. Title
PS3556.R352
813.54

Dedication

For Gaddy

Chapter 1

When Cosmo Greco learned of the layoff, the first thought that popped into his head was how he'd spend the rest of his day between the comic book store and the café. He blamed his apathetic response on not being fully awake, and blamed his fatigue on the barista whom he suspected had accidentally given him decaf instead of regular. In fact, he had been so tired that when he arrived in his staff area and noticed his colleagues shoving the contents of their desks into boxes he didn't question why they were doing this. He just went to his desk, sat down and checked his email as he did every day. The message that told of the layoff was highlighted with a bold red explanation point, indicating its urgency. Now, the disruptive atmosphere in the office made sense. As he was processing this connection, his boss, Pete, appeared at his desk, slouching over the gray fabric partition intended to provide Cosmo with a sense of privacy. Pete tried to appear remorseful by making a frown with his lips, but Cosmo could see delight shine through his beady eyes.

"So sorry about the layoff, Cosmo," he said in an unconvincingly sad voice. Cosmo knew that Pete approached him in hopes of seeing him upset by the layoff. Pete had resented Cosmo from the first day they met, a little over eight years ago, when the company hired him at the age of twenty. Pete viewed Cosmo as someone who slacked off at the very tasks in which he, himself, struggled.

"Well, thanks Pete," Cosmo said, looking at his former boss with a sincere expression. Pete never would have expected such a response. He might have expected something sarcastic or cynical, but nothing gracious. He furled his brows as if confused. Cosmo got great satisfaction from confusing Pete, and he'd miss playing the silent war game the two had played for eight years—a game which Cosmo had always won. Even now, Pete walked away from his desk, defeated.

As Cosmo stared at his desk, he thought it might look better to him now that he knew he wouldn't be sitting at it much longer, but it looked just as bland as ever. An off-white slab of plastic taken over by dirty coffee cups, pens—half of which didn't work—crumbled up aluminum wrappers from candy bars, stray papers, Post-it notes, inter-office manila envelopes, and an economy-sized bottle of Aleve to relieve his daily headaches. A dying plant sat on the edge of it as if wanting to fall off. He couldn't throw it out because his mom had given it to him. The only part of his desk that looked better than usual was his twenty-seven inch high definition monitor. Oh, how he loved to play games on that computer.

He got up to talk to his colleague Dario about the layoff. Dario's desk was on the other side of the staff kitchen, where Cosmo stopped to get a cup of coffee.

"Hey, Dario," Cosmo said as he approached his desk. He still wasn't feeling much about the layoff, but tried to act sad in support of Dario. He took a big gulp from his coffee, hoping that the caffeine would wake him up so that he could feel less apathetic.

"Hey," Dario said without looking up as he continued to clear out his desk. He hid behind a pair of big-rimmed glasses and his black hair, which hung like string beans in front of his face.

"Do you know how many of us got laid-off?"

"I don't know. I can't say that I care either."

"It's only a lay off," Cosmo said, surprising himself by his optimistic remark. "It could be temporary."

"Yeah right."

"You never know."

"Sometimes you do."

"You'd think seniority would count for something,"

"You'd think," Dario said, who seemed incapable of being shaken out of his cynicism.

Cosmo went back to his desk to pack, and as soon as he sat down, a wave of questions flooded his mind. What would he do now? What about health insurance? What if he got sick? Really sick? How tough was it going to be to get another job? Would he have to buy a suit in which to go on interviews? What would he put on his résumé? Should he take his dying plant home and try to resuscitate it?

He squashed the questions down so that he could pack up and get out of there. When he finished packing, he said goodbye to Dario and a few other colleagues. He took the elevator to the gray granite lobby where Muzak played loudly. He walked out the door and almost collided with someone. His near collision shook away any remnants of worry over his job loss, and as soon as he stepped out of the building, he felt as free as a bird that had escaped captivity from a small cage. An oak tree sat on the other side of the street—it must have been there for as long as he worked at the building but he had never noticed. Its leaves were yellow and orange with the slightest bits of green coming through in spots.

The tree made him want to see more trees. He wanted to see all of the trees that the city could show him, so he walked home through a part of the West Philadelphia neighborhood filled with trees and the scent of fall. It was part of the University of Pennsylvania campus called Locust Walk. He saw lots of trees in every color of the autumn rainbow. He walked slowly so he could stare at each one for as long as possible, almost as if to save the image of every tree and every leaf in his brain.

As he walked, he felt a slight bounce in his step. Not long ago, he walked with a big bounce in his step, his head bobbing back and forth as if to a song. In recent years, the bouncing and bobbing had faded, and he was glad to feel this part of him returning. Still, his head stayed stationary, and he wondered if it was static out of being uncomfortable, with a baseball cap that sat tightly upon it. He wore a hat to constrain his black, curly, wild hair but it popped out in places as if wanting to break free. He never left home without a hat. He kept one on even when he had a headache. As he passed a trashcan, he felt tempted to take it off and throw it out, but something in him wouldn't let him take it off. The hat did serve the purpose of keeping his hair out of his eyes so that his view of the trees was unobstructed.

As he looked at the trees, he remembered how he loved fall as a child. Fall meant school was starting, and school meant learning, and gathering knowledge was what he loved to do most in the world. He'd get excited each fall when he'd first notice a leaf that had changed its color. And even though he knew that the leaves changing colors meant that they were dying, he never felt death in the air. He felt life, renewal, and revival.

Cosmo skipped the comic book store and the café because he was so hungry by the time he got out of the office that he wanted to go straight home for lunch. He sat down to eat in front of the television set, as he did for all the meals he ate in his apartment. But today, for some reason, it felt wrong. He went back into his kitchen and sat at his table, staring at the refrigerator. It struck him that he should be looking at something else as he ate, and that his table was in the wrong position. It should face the window. There wasn't much of a view out his kitchen window. It was only the side of a brick building, but it was certainly more interesting than the refrigerator. So he moved his table and sat listening to the sound of the refrigerator hum.

He looked around at the apartment he had lived in for almost eight years. He hadn't noticed how chipped the paint was on his living room walls until now. Perhaps the sunlight pouring into the room was what made him notice the chipped paint. Usually, he had the curtains closed tight, making the room dark and all of its imperfections invisible. Today, he wanted them open. In the light, he could see more than just the chipped paint. He could also see all of the dust particles that floated in the air. He could see how crookedly his star maps were tacked to his walls; how his floor was almost completely covered with clothes, shoes, and books; and the dilapidated and worn condition of his furniture that looked as if he got it from the street. He could smell the stale, musty smell that permeated every inch of the place. He felt dirty just being here.

He had to clean his apartment right now! He began by wiping his furniture down with an old sock. After he had dusted, he picked up clothes from the floor, either putting them away or tossing them into the laundry. All of the drawers of his bureau were half-open, clothes coming out as if they wanted to escape the overcrowded drawers. He pushed down the clothing in his drawers and shoved them closed. He swept his worn down hardwood floors, wiped down the kitchen appliances and countertops, and tackled the bathroom last.

After cleaning, Cosmo sat and looked at his apartment feeling a sense of satisfaction. Unfortunately, he didn't get to experience this feeling long before all those disturbing questions about jobs, résumés and money reinvaded his head. He tried to make a plan about what to do first but his mind was going in too many directions, so he got up to get a pen and paper. As he did this, he heard a knock on his door. It was his younger sister, Silvia, looking more disheveled than he had ever seen her with clothing that looked like it came out of a trashcan and her hair a big mess of frizz and untamed curls. They had the same hair, with his being a few shades darker. They had the same big dark eyes that got a crazy glint in them on occasion. They had the same Romanesque shaped nose and the same slight built, but he stood about a foot taller than her at a little over six feet.

"You're here." She said this more like a question than a statement. It was two in the afternoon on a weekday, so he should not have been home. He should have been at work.

"So are you," he said, just as mystified about her presence as she was about his. "Why?"

"I might ask the same," she said as she walked past him and sat down on his couch. She looked around as if she didn't recognize the place. "Did you clean?"

"Yeah." The short-lived feeling of pride that he had had earlier for having done such a great cleaning job returned.

"Mm," she said, looking around with an approving face.

"So, what are you doing here?"

"Dad's driving me fucking crazy," she said. She had moved in with their dad, Frank, about six months ago, out of sheer desperation. No money. No job. No place to live. Frank was just about impossible to live with, and Silvia was living with him all alone. No other member of their family had ever had to bare such a feat. Their mom, Donna, had left him right before Silvia moved in and soon after she moved in, their youngest brother, Vince, was off to college.

Cosmo really felt for her being stuck in the house with Frank alone. But maybe it was for the best that she was coming to terms with reality now. She had planned on getting a teacher certification at a college not far from Frank's house in the spring, and she planned on living with their dad while she was in school. The plan was ridiculous, and he had told her so. He never hesitated to tell her just what he thought.

"You're out of your mind!" he said.

"But I think he's changing. Really." She sounded as if she was trying to convince herself of Frank's transformation as she was so inclined to do.

"Yeah," replied Cosmo, unconvinced. He looked over at her now, wondering whether or not she had finally learned that Frank wasn't changing, and probably never would change.

"So you took off from work?" Silvia said.

"Not exactly. I got laid-off."

"Oh, shit," she said without much urgency. "Sorry about that." But she didn't sound sorry. There was no remorse in her voice. She sounded relieved or even happy about his lay off. He tried to look at her face to see if he could verify what he thought he heard. But he could barely see her. Her puffy mess of curls and frizz hid her face. He couldn't read her body language either because she wore a black overcoat that appeared to be several sizes too big on her tiny body.

"So, what now?" she said, still not making eye contact.

"Look for another job," he said, as if the answer to her question should have been obvious.

"Are you still interested in driving to Portland with me by any chance?" She turned to him to reveal a spark of hope in her eyes. He should have known she was planning something. She always was. He returned her look of hope with a cynical expression, scrunching his face up like a prune, and didn't bother answering her question. He knew his little sister all too well. He knew that she'd abandon her idea to start school in South Jersey, want to move someplace far away, and want him to come with her, or at least drive with her. His being laid-off was the missing piece of the puzzle for her, and she probably figured the universe had made it happen to accommodate her plan. Now he understood why she seemed happy when he told her the news. After about a full minute of silence, she must have figured there was no response from him coming.

"Hell, why not just move out there with me? What are you staying in this shithole for anyway? There's nothing here for you? No job, no girlfriend, nothing! You'll love it out there! I just know it. It's beautiful, and people are there because they want to be there. Not because they're stuck there. And...."

"I don't feel stuck," Cosmo said with confusion in his voice as though he were asking his sister instead of telling her that he didn't feel stuck. She must have detected the uncertainty in his voice, for she raised her eyebrows and bore a smug look of satisfaction. She said nothing, which was worse than rambling on as she usually did.

"Maybe you're the one who feels stuck," he said.

"Yeah, I sure do feel stuck! I'm living with our crazy, alcoholic, raging dad and working at a candy shop in the mall."

"What about school? I thought you were going to start school in the spring. You're giving up on it just like that?"

"I'm not giving up on anything. Just because I move to Portland doesn't mean I can't go back to school."

Cosmo wasn't about to indulge in yet another conversation with Silvia about her moving around from place to place; how she was unable to stay in one place longer than a few months at a time; how she was always starting over. She might, after all, be growing up because she had been able to stay at Frank's house for almost half of a year. That would be a great accomplishment for anyone but especially for the restless and mobile Silvia. Six months in the same place could be considered 'settled down' for her.

"So, Portland, huh?" Cosmo said, prompting Silvia to talk some more about this place.

"Yeah, and it would be a great time for me to move out there now. My friend, Emily, needs a roommate. Her roommate moved out. Of course, if you decide to stay, we could get our own place. It's getting more expensive, but it's still affordable. Or at least more affordable than other cities."

As she rambled on about her plans for both of them, her voice became more and more distant until he could barely hear her at all. He was always amazed at how ready his sister was to make plans for other people, especially for him, regardless of his feelings against them. She'd plug people into her plans, as if plugging an exponent into a mathematical equation. He got up in the middle of her monologue to get a cup of tea from the kitchen. She didn't stop talking. She just followed him into the kitchen without any hesitation, speaking so fast that her words ran into each other. She had gotten to the part in her plan when they found an apartment and Cosmo was job hunting.

"I don't think you'll have any problem getting a job either. In fact, it'll probably be easier there than here. With so many people moving there now and...."

This was where he cut her off. Despite his secret relief in losing his job that morning, jobs were still a sensitive subject, one he didn't want to think about right now.

"Enough already, Silv," he said. "I'll think about driving out with you, but that's all."

Her rambling came to an abrupt halt, which was a great relief for Cosmo, who then suggested they go out for a drink. At this suggestion, Silvia's face squished up in confusion.

"I'm thoroughly grossed out by booze, and if you still lived with Dad, you'd be too."

"Well then, let's go out for coffee. Something. I just want to get out."

"That's weird," Silvia said. "You never want to get out." She looked suspicious and delighted at the same time and took her brother up on the offer.

◄►

Although the atmosphere of the café was different than that of Cosmo's apartment, the conversation remained the same. More of Silvia talking about how great Portland was. Cosmo was tempted to make some blunt, insensitive remark about how she couldn't stay still, and about how she'd get out there to discover that the place wasn't perfect and would then run back to

Jersey. But he kept his mouth shut. Last time he'd made such a remark, she stormed out of his apartment like a bolt of angry lightning. So he sat there and let her talk.

As she talked, he yawned and looked around the café, wishing to be involved in more interesting conversation. Silvia didn't seem to mind her brother's blatant disinterest. She was probably used to this sort of reaction from him. She knew he lacked social skills. He also knew he lacked social skills, and he didn't care one bit for improving that skill set. So as she talked on, he looked around at the café where he got a cup of coffee and a pastry to go every morning before work. He never sat inside prior to this afternoon. He never noticed the smell of coffee that filled the air, the paintings displayed on the walls, the fans attached to the high ceilings, the bright, stained glass tops of the walls. Most of all, he never noticed the cute girl who worked behind the counter. He stared right at her as if he were invisible. She had black almond-shaped eyes and wore overalls and her hair in braids. He wondered how he never noticed her before. But then, he never noticed anything in this place before.

"Cosmo, have you heard a word I've said?" Silvia said as if she suddenly cared that her brother wasn't listening.

"No," he said with complete indifference.

Silvia rolled her eyes and got up to put some more honey in her tea, giving Cosmo an opportunity to go back to staring at the cute girl in overalls. The girl caught him eventually, forcing him to look away. He used to not care about being caught and even encouraged it, as getting caught would be an opportunity. But now he couldn't even remember the last time he stared at a woman.

"You're checking that girl out," Silvia said, smiling as she sat down at the table. "That's a new one."

He just stared back at her, slanted lips, eyes jaded as if to tell his sister that her little remark wasn't so clever.

"There're lots of cute hipster girls in Portland, you know," she said, disregarding her brother's sarcastic expression.

"I told you I can't stand hipsters," he said, sipping his coffee that had grown cold.

"Well there're a lot of cute unhip girls there too, I'm sure."

"You still haven't been there yet, right?"

"Yeah, but I know enough about it to know I'd like it, and I know you would too, Cos," she said in a pleading voice.

When he tried to consider whether or not he'd like Portland, his mind went blank. He wasn't sure if he even liked Philadelphia. He had lived in this city for over ten years now, ever since he started school at the University of Penn. When he first arrived, he lived in a student apartment with two other roommates. He remembered all kinds of incidental details like the color of his kitchen chairs in his first apartment, but nothing about how he felt about the place.

"How could you know that? I don't even know that," he said knowing his attempt to be sensible was in vain.

"Well, you know you don't like it here, right?"

"I don't know that either."

"Do you like it here?"

"I don't know!" When those words came from his lips, he got a heavy, sad feeling.

Cosmo usually played video games until he fell asleep but tonight playing games was the last thing he wanted to do. He tried reading a comic book, but his attention drifted away after each caption. So he remained awake, looking up at the ceiling of his bedroom, noticing the cracks he had never seen. He wondered if he had too much time on his hands now, and if that was the reason for his noticing all the imperfections of his world. But he had only been laid-off for one day.

He got up to turn off his light, hoping the darkness might help him fall asleep, but the outside sounds of sirens, cars, and voices kept him awake. Usually, the city sounds never bothered him. But tonight the outside noise joined with the noise in his head, and together they made a symphony of cacophony. He thought of what he might do tomorrow, and then he thought of what he might do the day after and the day after that. He had to file for unemployment. That would be the first thing to do. Job hunting would be next, but where would he start? He never interviewed for a job. His last job was something he fell into right after he dropped out of college, when the economy wasn't falling apart; a time before well-qualified jobless people roamed the streets like hungry zombies. He had to get together a résumé. He couldn't imagine himself doing such a thing. He never had to make one. He thought he might ask Silvia for help. She must have been good at getting

jobs. She had no problems ever getting a job. Her problem was keeping one.

He tossed and turned with thoughts flying around his
head until two in the morning, at which time it began to
rain, which brought him a huge relief. The sound of rain
always put him to sleep.

The next morning, Cosmo's phone alarm went off
the same way it did every morning. And he obeyed the
alarm the same way he did every morning, slumping out
of bed like a reluctant turtle. He went into the kitchen
to make coffee and was midway through the process by
the time he remembered he had been laid-off yesterday.
He heard his sister waking up, stretching, and groaning
as if she hadn't slept enough.

"Hey, Cosmo," she shouted out to him because he
was still in the kitchen. "How did you sleep?"

"Not so good," he said, coming into the living room.
He heard the sound of something being slipped under
his door and looked down to see a small envelope. He
picked it up and opened it. It was a letter from the

building manager, declaring there'd be a ten percent increase in rent at the end of next month.

"Well, this sucks," he said. "Bastard's raising my rent. Oh shit, I can't catch a break!" He sounded like Frank complaining.

Silvia said nothing and Cosmo was grateful for her keeping her mouth shut. It would have been a perfect opportunity for her to talk about what a great time it would be for him to get out of Philly, to check out a new place, to see what else was out there. In addition to saying nothing, she had a look of sympathy on her face.

Why was this all happening now? If he believed in fate or destiny or any of those contrived philosophical concepts, he might think the universe was trying to tell him something. But he believed every person paved their own path, that nothing outside of himself could push him in any certain direction. He knew Silvia believed in all that nonsense and that she probably thought that the universe was trying to tell him something.

"I know what you're thinking," Cosmo said, sitting down on the couch.

"What?" she said, as if she had no idea what he was talking about.

He looked back at her as if to say "Don't waste your time pretending."

"All right, so what if I am thinking that this would be the perfect time for you to get out of town. So fucking what? You know I'm right." And then she said she had to dash off for work and left him alone with his thoughts, depriving him of an opportunity for a rebuttal to her last remark. So he sat there thinking of what he might have said if he had had the opportunity. But he couldn't think of any good comebacks. Maybe she had something. Maybe it would be a good time for him to check out a new place. He wouldn't have gone so far as to say a 'perfect' time, and he wouldn't have subscribed to her silly theory of the universe trying to tell him something. If the universe was telling him anything, it was that he had better get the unemployment application complete and start looking for a new job today.

It was late afternoon when Cosmo realized he had forgotten to eat all day. He went in the kitchen and opened his refrigerator to find a nearly empty container of milk, jars of condiments, and a carton of eggs with an expired expiration date. He was glad when he spotted a hunk of Swiss cheese and was grateful that it wasn't moldy. He had a can of olives and some stale bread that he revived by toasting. He ate his lonely meal of bread, cheese, and olives staring out his kitchen window at the brick wall of the apartment building next door.

After eating, he finished the unemployment application and started his résumé. He knew he should get busy job hunting but couldn't bring himself to do it. Maybe out of fear for what he'd find or not find. He thought of the note from his landlord that should have given him some feeling of urgency to start looking for jobs, but thoughts of his rising rent seemed to have a reverse effect upon him. Instead of feeling energized, he wanted to go back to bed and sleep for a long time. Maybe he could sleep as long as Rip Van Winkle and wake up with a new life, in a new world. And just as he walked into his bedroom for more sleep, his phone rang. It was Silvia and she told him she had given her boss notice and that she was going to Portland.

"So I'm going whether you come or not," she said in a very determined voice, "And I think you should come.

I'll even pay for your plane ride back. And I'm taking Interstate 40, so we'll pass right by the Grand Canyon. You can see the Grand Canyon, for Christ's sake!"

When he imagined the two of them riding out west, he felt less tired. Then he thought of something he wanted to see even more than the Grand Canyon, something just east of the Canyon. One of largest meteorite craters in the world.

"There's something I'd rather see even more. I want to see this crater that's just, like, thirty miles east of the Grand Canyon."

"Then we'll go there too," Silvia said, who probably would have agreed to anything.

"All right. I'll go." It was as if he was a ventriloquist's puppet having words placed in his wooden mouth. "Only for the drive though," he continued. "I'm not moving out there. So don't get any ideas."

As soon as he hung up the phone, his body filled with fear and questions. Who was this adventurous person who had taken over him and agreed to go? A feeling of excitement was struggling to get through, but his panic kept pushing it down. What was he afraid of anyway? He didn't know. As he tried to figure out why he was afraid of taking this trip, a vision of Donna came into his mind. In his vision, her face, which normally looked worried, appeared relaxed. She'll be greatly relieved to know her petite young daughter will not be driving cross-country alone, but that he'd accompany her. He was being a good older brother, and now pride got thrown into the mix of feelings.

In addition to being a good brother to his little sister, he also thought this trip might be just what he needed to clear his mind and realize what a good thing he had here, even with a rent hike and no job. He had a life here and that was more than he could say for lots of other people, including Silvia. After experiencing how his restless, nomadic sister lived her life, he'd be running back to Philadelphia.

Chapter 2

Cosmo was glad to be leaving his apartment a clean place rather than the dirty, dingy place it had been all the years he had lived there. He planned to return right after he dropped off Silvia in Portland, so imagined he'd be gone for one week at the most. One week wasn't a long time, but it was the longest he had ever been away from this place. He'd miss it even though he had grown sick of it. Silvia had insisted on picking him up at seven in the morning, so he woke at six. He couldn't recall ever seeing his apartment in such early morning light. The gray walls that had at one time been white looked brighter than usual. In fact, the whole place looked brighter than usual, and he took a good, long look at it in hopes of remembering the brighter version of his old worn down place.

He stuffed an army-green duffle bag he'd had since college, full with clothes and paperback books. Silvia would be coming by any minute to pick him up and then they'd be off. A feeling of slight nausea came over him when he heard her horn beeping outside his window. He looked outside to see that she was double-parked, so he knew that he had better hurry. He was glad he had to hurry in hopes that the bad feeling in his stomach would dissipate once he started moving, but it seemed to get bigger as he left his apartment, locked the door behind him, and ran down the steps. He felt like an invisible force was trying to pull him back as he ran past the faded lime green rugs and chipped painted walls of the hallway of his building. He hoped Silvia would be her usual preoccupied self, wrapped up in her own world so she could take him out of his world. She was. He was halfway in the car when she began with her itinerary for the day.

"We have to go back to Dad's," she said making the sickness in his stomach grow. "I forgot my phone, of all things. I was just over the bridge when I realized."

"Fuck," Cosmo said expressionless.

"Dad might not be there," she said in an effort to console her brother. Frank worked as a judge in a local courthouse, so because he didn't work a regular nine to five, Monday through Friday job, there was a chance he could be home on this particular weekday. And sure enough when they arrived, Frank's car was in the drive-way. He sat at the kitchen table having his morning drink of coffee, cream, and Sambuca. Cosmo never saw his dad look as bad as he did now. His eyes were sad, lost, and scared as he sat hunched over his drink as if it was all he had left in the world.

"Hi, Cosmo," he said in a tired, old, grumbled voice. He looked up at his son with his eyes but kept his head tilted down with his hand over his head as if it ached. Cosmo opened his mouth to respond to Frank, but no sound came out, almost as if he had forgotten how to talk. Maybe all the sympathy he felt for Frank made him go speechless.

"Hey, Dad. How's it going?" Cosmo was glad he could manage to say something, but sorely regretted asking the second he uttered these words. It was obvious Frank was in bad shape, and he had always been too willing to divulge his true state of being with anyone and everyone at any given time.

"Not too good," Frank said, without lifting his head to look up at his son, as if he didn't have the energy or strength to do so.

Cosmo was used to seeing his dad shuffling around the kitchen as if he were dancing to a polka song, drink in one hand, using the other to open and slam shut cabinet doors, taking frequent breaks to scream at his family or to make phone calls. He imagined his polka dance had slowed down to a slow waltz. He couldn't recall ever seeing him mope around like a depressed, lost soul, and this unfamiliar version of his dad made him confused and uncomfortable. He thought he might prefer to see him as his usual tyrant self. His feeling of discomfort grew when Silvia came into the kitchen to announce she couldn't find her phone. Great! Now they'd be there all morning and maybe even into the afternoon.

"Do you want something to eat?" Frank asked Cosmo with a glimmer of hope in his eyes. He might have been hopeful that his son would have some of his home-cooked food, especially now that they might be there for a while. Cosmo didn't trust Frank's food. No one did.

He'd cook meat that had been frozen, defrosted, and re-frozen again, drench his vegetables in oil that may or may not have been way past its expiration date, and use too much pepper on everything. Silvia suspected that this was to cover up the taste of whatever he cooked. When Cosmo lived at the house, he always had an excuse ready as to why he couldn't eat his dad's food. Frank was smart enough to know he was being lied to though, and his feelings that seemed incapable of being hurt would be hurt by his son's refusal to eat his food. At the time, Cosmo couldn't have cared less about hurting Frank's feelings, but now that he was feeling sorry for him, he felt that taking his dad up on his offer was the right thing to do.

"Sure," Cosmo said with slight fear in his voice. "I already ate, but I can eat something small." He lied. He hadn't eaten anything yet that day and was starving. He hoped his dad would make him something like some toast with butter, but he had no such luck. Frank rose from his seat as if he had a reason to live again and got a bunch of ingredients out of the refrigerator. By the looks of the ingredients, he'd be making one of his famous frittatas.

Cosmo felt a great sense of relief at seeing his dad getting back to his usual self. This was the Frank he could visualize raising hell and screaming at him, "You're nothing but a failure, and you'll never amount to anything!" Now he could go back to the more comfortable, familiar feeling of anger toward his dad.

But something was wrong. He couldn't seem to feel anger toward him, almost as if there was something inside him blocking the feeling. He kept seeing Frank's sad, lost, puppy-dog eyes instead of the mean, scary eyes he normally wore on his face. His sympathy for his dad was so great, in fact, that he brought himself to compliment the frittata. It wasn't such a terrible lie. Besides being too oily, it wasn't so bad. "Mmm. Good eggs," he said. Cosmo rarely gave flattery, and never gave false flattery, so he surprised himself by being able to do it with relative ease. When he saw the smile on his dad's face as a result, he felt his phony flattery might have been a good thing.

"The potatoes came out good too, huh?" Frank asked with a look of pleading in his eyes, as if his survival was dependent on his son liking his cooking.

"Yeah, great," Cosmo said, causing his dad's face to brighten.

The exchange might have been the closest thing to a conversation that they ever had in their lives. Frank wasn't one for conversation. He typically talked at people, not allowing any space for dialogue. But at this moment, it looked as if he might invite some conversation from Cosmo, who struggled in his mind thinking of what to say next. Then Silvia popped her head into the kitchen to say that she still hadn't found her phone.

"I'll try calling you," suggested Cosmo.

"It's no good," Silvia said. "I turned the ringer off."

Cosmo wondered if his sister had planned this whole thing. She had been trying to make peace between her dad and brother for a while now, and maybe this was her way of getting them together before she ran off to Portland. He wanted to be angry with his sister for being her usual, plotting self, but how could he be angry with her for trying to do something good, even if it was underhanded? That was Silvia's style.

He glanced over at his dad, who looked as if he had returned to being depressed. "I guess I'll be all alone now." He talked and sounded like Eeyore the donkey and almost made Cosmo want to encourage his sister to stay. But he couldn't do that to her. He knew only too well how fast Frank could change into another person. Still, he needed to say something consoling. He could have never imagined himself wanting to give his dad consolation.

"What about Angie? Maybe you can visit her." This was the only thing Cosmo could think of saying. Angie was Frank's favorite. Surely, the thought of seeing her would bring him some comfort.

"She's all the way up in North Jersey," Frank said, even more discouraged. And then he repeated one of his favorite phrases: "I'll be all alone like a dog." It was no use telling Frank anything. Words bounced off him. Angie lived only about an hour and a half away from Frank, but as far as he was concerned, she might as well live on another planet. He didn't like to go outside of the general vicinity of South Jersey. He didn't even like to go outside of his little town.

Cosmo thought of his sweet old Uncle Nick, Frank's brother, who seemed to have more patience and love for Frank than anyone. There was something saintly about the man. And he only lived about a half hour away.

"Why don't you go visit Uncle Nick?" Cosmo said. At this, Frank got the slightest bit of hope in his eyes, and he nodded as if to say that it was a good idea. But in a flash, the sad part of him took over, and he went back to slumping before his drink. The strength of his sadness and discouragement seemed to outweigh any sort of hope and light that tried to come into his body. Just then, Frank's phone, which was right next to his drink, rang a full two rings before he answered it. This was unusual for him. He was always answering the phone as soon as it rang, sometimes before it even had a chance to complete one ring.

"Oh, it's Angie," he said through a strained smile as he looked down at his phone.

Cosmo never thought he'd feel glad to hear that Angie was calling. The two had been in conflict since childhood. She was Frank's favorite, and Cosmo was his least favorite. In addition to that, they were completely different from each other. Cosmo couldn't care less what people thought of him. Angie cared too much about what people thought of her.

"Why don't you come down and see me?" Frank said to Angie with heaviness and longing in his voice. Cosmo could hear his sister, through the phone, giving some excuse that involved her toddler daughter, Isabella, and he thought of how great it must be to have a constant excuse like a small child.

"Here, talk to your brother," Frank said all of a sudden. "I have to go to the bathroom." Frank was always giving the phone to whoever happened to be in the room without regard for whether or not the two people wanted to talk to each other. Cosmo didn't want to talk to Angie, and he was sure she wouldn't want to talk to him.

"Hey, Angie," Cosmo said, dumbfounded by his dad's gesture.

"Hey. How's it going?" Angie asked without much interest in her voice. She had married rich, and although Cosmo had never been to her house, he had heard about it from Silvia. He imagined his beautiful sister sitting like a princess on some designer leather sofa in a posh room that was three times the size of his entire apartment.

"I'm all right. How's everything up there?" For a fraction of a second, he contemplated what it would be like to tell her honestly how it was going. His relationship with Angie was anything but honest. They had built their relationship on lies and struggle; on who was winning and who was losing; on who was wrong and who was right. It left no room for things like honesty. Sometimes he wished he didn't have to keep up the silly facade that started when they were children, but he couldn't imagine starting over now, and he couldn't see how all the bad between them could be undone. It grew and became more complicated with each passing year.

He had an opportunity to resolve their conflict about three years ago when Angie had asked him to be godfather of Isabella. He sometimes wished he had accepted the offer to be her daughter's godfather. He told her and everyone in the family that he couldn't accept this honor due to his lack of any religious affiliations. But that was only an excuse for the real reason he didn't want to be Isabella's godfather. He didn't want to sew up the hole between him and his sister. It was easier to let it widen, and with Cosmo, the easier option usually won. When he considered being Isabella's godfather, he knew it would require him to be in contact with Angie, to go visit her at her estate home in North Jersey, to be on a friendly basis with her annoying husband, Doug, to remember to buy Isabella birthday and Christmas gifts, and to be present for all the little girl's parties. When he tried to imagine himself doing any of that, he knew he couldn't pull it off. He was a lot of things, but never a fake.

"Oh, I've been good," she said. "Busy, but good." Cosmo couldn't imagine what she could be busy doing. She didn't need to work, and she had enough money to buy all the services she needed. Then she went on to explain that Isabella was starting pre-school and that she was doing a lot of volunteering at the school.

"Mmm," Cosmo said trying to conceal his disinterest. He was relieved when Frank came in the kitchen and he could hand the phone back to him. "Hey, well, here's Dad," Cosmo said. "Nice talking to you."

He gave the phone back to Frank and looked at the clock on the stove, realizing that forty minutes had passed since he had been sitting in the kitchen of the home where he grew up. The kitchen looked the same in terms of the layout with its big wooden table in the center of the room surrounded on all sides by all the things a kitchen needed. But the old room screamed of neglect. The floor looked warped from moisture, as it was protruding in spots. The wood on the cabinets was chipped and worn. The door of the closet looked as if it could fall from its hinges at any second. One or more of the drawers didn't close straight, but tilted, revealing an opening. The refrigerator hummed loudly, and the sink leaked. He had an urge to check out his old room, but kept himself from doing it. He was afraid to see what it had become. He assumed it was the most neglected of all of the rooms in the house.

He wanted to scream out to Silvia to ask her if she had found her phone yet, but he said nothing. He just continued sitting there as if mute and incapacitated, feeling sad for the kitchen that was once home to so many good times. He thought of dyeing Easter eggs in the spring. His Christmas Eve dinners when Donna would make seven different kinds of fish. He thought of Sunday dinners that lasted all day. And then a bunch of bad memories flooded his head. The time Frank turned the table over in one of his Incredible Hulk rages. The time he splattered a tray of blueberry buckle on the floor. And worst of all, the time he hit Donna. Cosmo wasn't in the kitchen at the time, or even in the house; he was away at college. But he felt he had been there, in a way, because he heard about it through Silvia and Vince, who were both home at the time. He felt less heavy with sorrow for the present day Frank as he thought of their tumultuous past, and he suddenly had the strength and will to call out to his sister.

"Hey, Silv," he said, "we got to get going. Did you find your phone yet?"

"Oh, yeah," Silvia said popping her head in the kitchen. "I found that a while ago. I was just going through some of my stuff to take with me."

Cosmo rolled his eyes at his sister, but his cynical facial expression turned to one of sadness as he glanced over at Frank, whose face was filled with desperation.

"You're leaving me," Frank said to Silvia, as if he were a child being dropped off on the playground for his first day of school. It looked as if he was about to start fake crying, which was something he saved for these sorts of occasions.

"I'll be back, Dad," Silvia said. Cosmo knew she was lying; she had no intention to come back. But knowing his sister, there was a good chance she'd be back. He predicted she'd make it to Portland and, shortly after finding a job and a place to live, she'd find something wrong with the place. She'd end up coming back to stay

with Frank because she'd be broke. He based his prediction on his experience of his sister for the past three
years since she had finished college.

Her attempt to console Frank was useless, and he
continued to stare out into space like an abandoned
puppy dog. Cosmo thought the look on his dad's face
might stay with him forever, making it more difficult
for him to be angry with Frank for calling him a good-
for-nothing failure while he was growing up. He could
barely remember the scary, ferocious dad he had known
all his life, as now he was nothing more than a big,
helpless, lonely child. At one time, he thought he might
enjoy seeing his dad in this kind of deteriorated state,
but he couldn't stand another second of it. He had such
a great urgency to console Frank that he said, "Dad, I
can come and visit you sometime."

At this, Frank's eyes filled with the kind of joy of a
child who had just entered an amusement park. "You
will? Oh, that'd be great. Just great." Cosmo looked over
to see his sister staring at him with a look of shock on
her face. He looked back at Frank, who stared at him as
if he was some sort of savior. He had never gotten that
sort of responses from anyone. And never would have

guessed in a million years that he could have gotten such a response from Frank. He also could have never envisioned himself rescuing Frank.

"Dad, why don't you call somebody?" Silvia said, who also seemed to be feeling bad for Frank. "Uncle Nick or your friend, Tony, or Joe. Maybe you can get out tonight."

"Okay," Frank said with a smile so strained that it looked almost painful.

Cosmo couldn't seem to pull himself away, so he decided to do it swiftly. And just like pulling a Band-Aid off, he was out of the door, Silvia following him, still consoling Frank as she walked away.

"Bye, Dad!" she said. "Love you!" And at these words, Frank gushed fake tears.

"I love you too," he said in his broken, crying voice. Cosmo struggled to remember all the times he screamed at her and kicked her out of the house, but couldn't. All he could see was the two of them parting ways like two people who loved each other deeply but needed to be separated by some artificial constraint, like a war or a prison sentence.

Cosmo didn't turn around because he knew that if he did, he'd see a version of his dad that would haunt him for the rest of his days. He couldn't wait to get away from Frank's house and get on the road, and he was delighted to have found a distraction as soon as he got into Silvia's car. He offered to drive and so he had to move the seat back and make all of the appropriate adjustments to the rear view mirrors. When he finished making these adjustments, he looked over at Silvia to see that she was still waving goodbye to Frank, but he dared not glance at the object of her waving. She had mastered the acting skill he had never achieved. He knew she was ecstatic inside about getting away from their dad, but she played the role of a heartbroken girl so well.

"Oh jeez, he's following the car now," she said sarcastically while still waving with a sad smile on her face. "I hope he finds a lady friend soon."

Cosmo figured it was easy for Silvia to be detached from the sad version of their dad, as she had just spent a long amount of time living with him. It wasn't actually that long, only a few months, but time with Frank had to be measured in dog years. So a few months was more like a few years. And her time counted even more because she lived alone with him. He was sure if he had done the same, he wouldn't be feeling an ounce of sympathy for Frank. He felt tempted to turn around and look at his dad one last time, but he restrained himself.

"I said I hope he finds a lady friend soon," she said, sounding bothered by Cosmo's lack of response.

"I heard you the first time," he said.

"Well, a response would be nice."

"Yeah, I agree." He felt his sister staring at him as if she wanted another, different response, or as if she wanted him to speak his response with more feeling.

"You feel bad for him, don't you?" She said this as if she had solved a great mystery of the universe. He didn't like that she always knew what was up with him, and he didn't bother responding to her question. Instead, he changed the subject.

"You've been riding the clutch. It feels worn."

"No, I haven't been. You didn't answer my question, which leads me to believe that you do feel bad for Dad." He could see her smiling out of the corner of his eye.

"So what if I do?"

She didn't say a word. She just sat there, but Cosmo could feel a great smugness emanating from her. He paid her no mind though. Instead, he was focused on looking around at his hometown that he hadn't seen in years. The center of town was only about four blocks long and three blocks wide, and although it looked mostly unchanged since last he saw it, there were some minor additions. He saw a café he hadn't seen before and new pizza place too. Still, it maintained that old style American town that had been lost in a country that had filled itself with strip malls and superstores in more recent decades. He saw the same bakery he used to get pizza at after school in fifth grade—a small building with a glass front. He then drove by the alley where he used to get high after school in his teen years. Not far from the alley, he was glad to see the army-navy store where he got his first job when he was seventeen years old. He was hired by a nice old man whose dad opened the store back in the fifties. He worked in the back of the store, unloading their few deliveries, straightening, keeping track of the merchandise. He liked the job, mostly because it kept him out of the house.

"Oh, shit!" Silvia said as they left the town. "I never said bye to Mom."

"Well, look at the time," Cosmo said pointing to the clock in the car, which said that it was nine o'clock. "We're not going to have time to make another stop. Besides, how do you know Mom is even around? She's probably at work." She worked as a professor at a college in South Jersey teaching English literature, and she lived, for the time, in a studio in the downtown section of Philadelphia.

"We have to go back over the bridge to get to 95 anyway," Silvia said in a coaxing voice. "Don't you have some kind of timeline?" Cosmo said as he opened the window to pay a toll. He was sure that she had some sort of deadline, some reason to rush to the other side of the country.

"Well, yeah, but it will only take a minute," she said as she got her phone out of her bag. "Let me at least see if she's around."

Before Cosmo knew it, his sister had reached his mom and they were making plans for a goodbye visit.

"All right," Cosmo said. "You have to give me directions, you know. When I go to see Mom, I take the bus, so I don't know how to get there by car."

"No problem," Silvia said in her most agreeable tone of voice.

———

Silvia's second sudden change of plans annoyed Cosmo, who showed his annoyance by not talking to his sister until they crossed the Ben Franklin Bridge.

"Which way?" he said as soon they got over the bridge.

"Take Vine to Broad to Lombard," she said without hesitation, leading Cosmo to believe she had driven to Donna's many times since their mom had moved from their former home. Donna had left Frank about a little over a half a year ago. Cosmo was surprised that she lasted as long as she did. Everyone was. But she was determined to wait until the youngest Greco, Vince, was out of the house before leaving Frank. She almost made it too. She left only a couple of months before Vince graduated high school. Cosmo was relieved, even happy, when his mom left his crazy dad and only wished that she had done it sooner. The happiness he got from this event faded a bit today after seeing such a pathetic version of Frank.

"I'll start looking for a spot now," Silvia said.

"We'll never find a spot here," he said in a frustrated voice. "We'll have to park in a lot." He knew Silvia, who was always broke and cheap, wouldn't be much into paying for parking, but he thought she should know better than to expect to find a street parking spot in the center of the city at this time of day. He imagined she parked her car in some terrible, far-away neighborhood and then walked for a couple of miles just to save a few bucks when she came to visit Donna.

"Can I get some money, please?" He turned to his sister when he entered the lot. She reluctantly gave him a ten-dollar bill, which he in turn gave to the parking lot attendant. He rolled his eyes at her while thinking about how potentially bad the whole money issue could play out on this trip.

"What?" she said in response to his rolling eyes.

"You seemed like you didn't want to give up that ten-dollar bill."

She said nothing, which was unlike her. She always had a response prepared and was always quick with her replies. Cosmo wondered how financially prepared she was to make this trip.

"You have enough money for this trip, right?" he said.

"Of course I do," she responded. But she said nothing else, which prompted Cosmo to say, "You know it can get expensive, and I just got laid-off, so I might have to watch my money."

"I know," she said as if this information was apparent to her, but Cosmo still felt uncomfortable, so he asked her how much money she had saved.

"Three thousand dollars," she said turning toward him. "That's how much, and it may sound like a lot, but I have to get myself all set up in Portland, and who knows how long it will be before I find a job, and...." He cut her off at this, as he knew she was never out of work. Silvia would clean the streets for money if she had to.

"I'm sure you'll have a job in no time, Silv." He said this with a partial laugh, remembering all the crazy jobs his sister had worked to earn a buck. One summer, she dressed up in a giant peanut costume and stood outside a salt-water taffy shop on a boardwalk at the shore, luring tourists into the taffy shop. He sometimes wished he had a little bit of her adaptable, free-spirited nature. He always did what was safe and sure and boring. His life seemed colorless and stale next to his sister's life.

She'd have stories to tell when she became old. What stories would he have? In addition to having stories, she had more money than he had too. He wondered how she had managed to save so much money. He didn't have that much money saved, and he worked the same boring job for years. He was bored and broke, and while she wasn't rich, she had more money than he had, and she appeared to have a more interesting life.

She got out of the car, going toward Donna's apartment building. She walked as if she were perpetually running late for something, quite different from how he walked. He took slow strides even if he were running late for something. And despite the fact that she was much shorter than he was, she always got to wherever they were going first. In this case, it was the elevator of Donna's building, which she held for him. She had an impatient look on her face, which made Cosmo walk even slower.

"What's wrong?" she asked her brother, pushing the elevator button for the third floor.

"Nothing," he said as if he didn't know what she was talking about.

"Well then, why are you going so slow? You know we have a big trip ahead of us." She said this as if the length of their trip was new information for him.

"Hey, you're the one who wanted to make another stop," he said snidely, as if he knew that he was irritating his sister.

When they arrived at Donna's door, Cosmo heard his mom scream, "Wait a minute! Be right there!" He heard the sound of a teapot whistling on the stove, and he imagined his mom rushing around her tiny studio apartment, getting prepared for their visit. She arrived at the door dressed in white, looking fresh and radiant. Her olive skin shone bright, her dark brown eyes were open wide. Since she had left Frank, it seemed as though she were aging backward. Cosmo thought he could almost see the lines on her face erasing over time. She was no longer the falling apart, broken-down woman Cosmo knew as his mom.

He was happy for her separation from Frank but upon this visit, he felt a twinge of sadness for his mom. Maybe because her entire apartment was one room. One small room. And it looked more like a hotel room than a place where a person lived. She had not changed

a thing about it since she moved in several months ago.
But it was something more than her apartment that
made him feel sorry for her. She was alone in this place.
He never felt sorry for himself for being alone. He liked
being alone. It was strange that he felt this way about
Donna now. She looked much better than when she
lived with Frank, so she must be happier and more at
peace than when she lived with him. But his mom never
divulged a bit of herself to anyone. She didn't even tell
anyone in their family that she was moving out or leaving Frank. It was just like her to keep her problems to
herself, not to let anyone, even her children, in.

"Are you hungry?" she asked as Cosmo and Silvia sat
down at the bar that was Donna's kitchen table. Cosmo
wasn't hungry after eating at Frank's house. In fact, his
stomach felt slightly sick. But still, he had no idea where
his next meal would be, and he imagined that if he were
lucky, it would be at a Denny's.

"I made some vegetarian lasagna last week and froze
the extra," she said, emphasizing the word 'vegetarian'
to Silvia, who was a non-meat eater. "I know it's a little
early for lasagna, but...." Donna didn't need to sell her
scrumptious cooking to anyone, let alone her children,

and before she could finish her sentence, Silvia said that she'd love some. Cosmo said he'd have only a small piece.

"He ate at Dad's," Silvia jumped in.

"You ate your dad's cooking?" Donna said, eyes and mouth both open wide.

"He was just being nice," Silvia said, not giving Cosmo a chance to answer for himself.

"It may have not been such a great idea either," Cosmo said with a look on his face enough to express a sick stomach.

"Well, maybe you can have some biscuits. Or crackers. Something to settle your stomach," Donna said. This appealed to Cosmo, and he said he'd have some.

"I'll get it all together quick," Donna said, getting her children's meals prepared. The act of making them something to eat seemed to give her some joy. He recalled all of the times Donna had rushed about the kitchen cooking dinner when Frank was around. Often, Frank would stick his nose into whatever she was making, as if he wanted to get the recipe but didn't have the courage to ask. Then a far-away memory of Donna cooking popped into his head. He was about ten years old, it was Valentine's Day, and Frank had bought

Donna a Russell Stover heart. Frank baffled Cosmo during such times. He could be so charming and there was a small but noteworthy part of him that had never stopped being in love with Donna and never stopped showing it. Before Cosmo could finish his reminiscence of a past Valentine's Day, Donna had their food ready and placed neatly on two plates in front of them.

"How's everything?" Donna asked as she sat down on a loveseat sofa that was about a foot outside of the kitchen area.

"It's great," Silvia said, taking a forkful of lasagna that looked too big for her.

"Yeah, I think these biscuits are helping," Cosmo said, dunking one in a cup of tea Donna got for him.

"So, Cosmo," Donna said. "You decided to go with Silvia to Portland?" She seemed surprised, as going on a cross-country trip wasn't in her son's character.

"Yeah," he said as if he hid nothing. "Should be a good time."

"And you were able to take a vacation from work with no problem?"

"Yeah," Cosmo said. He was grateful that Silvia didn't look in his direction or do anything that might lead

Donna to believe he was lying. Instead, his sister cleverly redirected the conversation.

"Want to see the route we're taking, Mom?" She said this while taking a map out of her backpack.

"I most certainly do," Donna said, standing up to see the map. "And I expect a phone call every night. Or at least a text." She had a type of maternal authority in her voice.

Silvia unfolded the map and showed her mom the highlighted route they'd be taking. Cosmo wondered why he, himself, didn't think of asking his sister about the route. Both he and Donna had the same reaction to Silvia's planned route. "It looks like the long way," Donna said.   "Yeah," Cosmo said. "Why are we taking the long way?"

"Well, for a few reasons," Silvia said as if she had anticipated this reaction. "First of all, I want to see Vince in Berkeley." She must have known that Donna would be in great favor of this idea, and when Cosmo looked over at his mom, he saw a gracious smile on her face. "And secondly, I have a friend in Memphis who we can stay with a night. And thirdly, we'll have an opportunity to see the Grand Canyon if we go this route."

"Wow, that's supposed to be something to see," Donna said with longing in her voice, as if she wished she were going on this ride with her children. She glanced over at Cosmo. "It's just a big hole," he said grinning, trying to make his mom feel all right about her missed opportunity.

"It's one of the seven natural wonders of the universe, Cosmo!" Silvia jumped on him.

"Hey, didn't you live in Arizona?" Cosmo said to Silvia. "How come you didn't see it when you lived there?"

"I lived in Tucson, the southeastern part of the state," Silvia said. "That's like really far from the Grand Canyon."

"So, did you want to make it to Memphis tonight?" Cosmo said, studying the map.

"Yeah, it's only about fifteen hours," Silvia said, as if fifteen hours was a trip around the corner. "My friend won't care if we make it to his place in the middle of the night."

"We're never going to make that," Cosmo said, stretching his hands out over his head.

"Oh yeah, we will," Silvia said, very sure of herself.

"Well then, we better get going," Cosmo said, getting up out of his seat to use the bathroom. He was sure he was right and Silvia was wrong, but he didn't see the use in arguing the point, especially with how sad she looked at the moment.

"You don't have to go, you know," Donna said to her daughter, undoubtedly seeing her sadness.

"I know, Mom," Silvia said, some reluctance in her voice. "I want to check it out though." She shrugged her shoulders and said, "You know me. I'll probably be back before you know it." It was obvious to Cosmo that she was only saying this to make their mom feel better, which she didn't achieve. Donna looked back at Silvia as if struggling to understand her daughter but failing at the task. As long as Cosmo could remember, she never did understand Silvia. Silvia was an impractical, ide-alistic artist type, and Donna was a pragmatist and a realist. Donna knew at a young age that she wanted to have four children and that she wanted to be a college professor. She set out to achieve her goals proactively with her two feet planted on the ground. Silvia flitted from one idea to the next, her head high in the clouds most of the time. It could have been the reason why the two of them had never been very close. Silvia was much closer to Donna's mom, Grandma Tucci. When their grandma died, it shattered little Silvia, who was in her young teen years at the time.

Cosmo left the sad scene to use Donna's tiny bathroom, and on his way back, he noticed a letter on top of the television set addressed to his mom from an attorney's office. He didn't need to speculate on what the envelope contained, as it was obvious it had something to do with her and Frank's divorce, which she initiated.

When he got back to his mom and sister, he noticed a light in his mom's face that he had not seen since he was a boy. Maybe the darkness he saw in Frank's face that morning was the tradeoff for the new light in his mom's face, and with that thought, he felt a sense of balance inside—not a feeling of happiness or sadness, but one of neutrality. He was happy that he could watch Silvia and Donna part ways without the same sinking feeling he had when he watched his sister and dad say goodbye. Despite his feelings of sympathy for his mom, he had confidence in her ability to be all right on her own. She contrasted Frank in her fierce independence, and Cosmo could envision his mom contentedly living alone in this little studio into her old age. Poor Frank was so needy and because of his neediness, nothing on the outside could ever be enough for him.

They headed out the door, and Donna told them for the fifth time to be sure to call her every night. She then grabbed her keys and said, "I'll come down with you." Cosmo knew his mom couldn't like the idea of her daughter leaving her to live across the country, but she made no indication of her feelings in her actions. It was more as if she pushed her away with lots of cautionary warnings, as opposed to Frank, who tried to pull her back with his sad eyes.

"I'll miss you, Mom," Silvia said, looking up at Donna.

"I'll miss you too, Silvie," Donna said. She still wasn't giving anything away except for more warnings. "Your car's in good shape, right?"

"Yeah," Silvia replied as if the answer should have been apparent.

"Don't forget to stop to check the tire pressure," Donna said, seeming to search herself for more warnings for her daughter. "You don't want to get a blowout."

"I know, Mom," Silvia said as she opened her car door.

"Okay, well, I hate long goodbyes," Donna said bending down to hug her daughter. She gave her a brief hug and said "I love you," as if she had no problem at all sending her off into the great beyond. It wasn't the first time, after all, and Cosmo was sure it wouldn't be the last.

Chapter 3

"**G**ot any other stops you want to make?" Cosmo asked Silvia, half joking, half serious, as he drove out of the downtown. Silvia didn't bother responding. Instead, she slanted her lips, rolled her eyes, and asked Cosmo if he knew the way to Interstate 95. He thought he should know the way, but he didn't. He hadn't owned a car in years, and even when he did have a car, he never left the city. Still, he didn't want to ask his younger sister for directions, so he said he'd pull over and look at the map. The map was useless in terms of the local area. It was only useful for major interstates. Philadelphia was no more than a dot.

"This map is useless," he said, handing it back to his sister. "Do you have any local maps?" At this, Silvia opened the glove compartment of her car, which appeared to have a special way of opening. She had to tap on its bottom while simultaneously pressing the lever. He imagined there were many other little tricks to his sister's car. By the looks of the rest of the car, it was apparent that she didn't like to change or fix things. She preferred to keep things broken and to find tricks to get around the car's broken stuff. The car itself appeared to be on its last legs, and it seemed as if Silvia was determined to get every bit of life that she could from the poor, old thing. It had lots of dents and scratches and had one of its front panels missing for as long as she had owned it. She had cleaned the interior to make room for her belongings, which included a couple of orange crates filled with clothes and painting supplies. But normally the floor was covered in used snot rags and empty food containers.

She opened the glove compartment to reveal a bunch of papers that had been jammed into it, and she pulled out a few maps and went through them, naming them as she went: "Arizona, Illinois, New York," she said. "No maps of this area though. Sorry. But like I said, I can give you directions to 95." She didn't seem to understand his need to look at a map.

"All right," Cosmo said. "Go ahead." She gave him step-by-step directions, and he was pleasantly surprised that she gave every part of the directions well in advance of each turn or move he had to make.

Within an hour of driving, they entered Delaware. It had a big blue sign that said 'Welcome to Delaware. It's good being first.' Cosmo stared at the sign as if he had never seen a welcome sign. Even though it was another lifetime ago, he should have seen some during his families' annual summer trips to Quebec, but he couldn't recall seeing any.

"Our first welcome sign," Silvia said, as if she was initiating him into her road world.

"Yeah," Cosmo said. "Hey, funny thing; I can't remember seeing any welcome signs when we'd take our family trips to Canada."

After a few seconds, Silvia said, "Me neither." She didn't sound nearly as curious as her brother was about recalling more about their family trips. "You never seemed too excited about those trips. Remember the year you got out of going?"

"Yeah. Sure do," he said. He was eighteen, old enough to stay home on his own. He thought of making a phony excuse to get out of going, but in the end, he decided to go the honest way. He told Donna he didn't want to go because being in the same car with Frank for such a long period made him uneasy. She showed sympathy for him in her eyes, and said in her most serious and somber voice, "I understand, Cosmo."

Inside, he was elated, but he masked his elation so he could appear defeated and broken to his mom. He thought he'd have a great time, escaping the trip and having the house to himself, bare of Frank. But he ended up regretting getting out of the trip. He felt a strange longing to be with his family during their annual trip. He found himself sitting around the house reminiscing about previous trips, thinking that they were not so bad after all. He thought he'd go next year for sure and was disappointed when Donna came home and said that may have been their last trip to Quebec.

"Why?" he asked his mom, confounded.

"Your dad," Donna said as she unpacked her belongings, putting them back in her closet as if she was angry at them. Cosmo needed no more explanation. He knew Silvia would fill him in on more of the details of the trip. And he was right.

"Well, first he did his usual thing where he pulls over to the side of the road just as we're all nearing the border and pretends like he's turning around, and says, 'I'm gonna turn this God damn car around back to New Jersey!'" Frank usually made this threat just as they neared their destination, and Cosmo always felt greatly relieved at the thought of turning back and going home. Silvia continued on with the events in what seemed to be in chronological order. "Right as we're approaching Montreal, we go for a picnic in the park, and Vince said something to set him off, and Dad chased Vince around the park. Vince ran away, and Mom found him hiding inside of one of these hollowed out trees in the park. The next night, we went out to dinner and of course, he went crazy when he saw the bill." She took a brief pause and looked up at the ceiling as if she was searching her mind for any other events, but she couldn't think of any.

"Maybe Mom is getting to the end of her rope," Cosmo had suggested.

"Probably," agreed Silvia.

The letter Cosmo saw from a lawyer's office in Donna's apartment flashed in his mind and he contemplated telling Silvia about it, but she looked so placid staring out the window and he didn't want to disturb her apparent tranquility. So instead he looked around at the state that he couldn't recall ever visiting. It was so close to where he lived, but there was never any reason for him to go there. It looked plain and bland and spacious—at least more spacious than the areas of Jersey and Philly that they had driven through this morning. The highway wasn't so jammed full of cars and trucks and there weren't many houses or buildings along the side of the road. Cosmo wished for an opportunity to stop there and see what it felt like outside of the car but they were through the tiny state in a flash and onto the next state.

Almost as soon as they entered Maryland, the scenery by the highway changed, filling with rolling hills, autumn-colored trees and occasional farms. They stopped at a rest stop about a half hour after entering at Silvia's request. The parking lot of the rest stop was packed with cars going in every direction. Silvia urged him to park far away from the tan building that contained the restrooms and eateries so they could get some exercise. He ignored her request.

"I hate when people park so close," she said waving her arm in the air. "Like it's going to kill you to get some exercise."

"I don't think ten steps really counts as exercise," Cosmo said, getting out of the car.

"Well, it might be all we get this week."

"When you drive, you can park far away from wherever we're going," he said, entering the rest stop.

He got a large coffee while she used the ladies' room and prepared himself for whatever lecture he'd be getting on the dangers of caffeine. To his surprise, she had no lecture. Rather, she said, "I wish you would have gotten me a coffee too."

"I thought you didn't drink coffee," he said, more a question than a statement.

"I do," she said, looking at the long line forming at the Starbucks stand. "Especially when I'm driving cross country. Do you mind if I get a cup?"

"No," he said drinking from his cup.

"Be back in two minutes," she said, running away from him.

Cosmo didn't mind waiting and looking around at the rest stop. It was packed, and the crowdedness of the place confused him. Autumn didn't seem like the time of year that so many people should be traveling on the road. All the people seemed to blur into each other and become one big mass of rushing energy. If he looked at any one of them individually, they looked alien to him. He had gotten so used to only seeing city people that he forgot about the existence of other types of people. This place was filled with suburbanites. He enjoyed watching them and feeling like an outsider and an observer, and before he knew it, Silvia was back with her coffee, and they were off. Shortly after getting back on the road, Silvia's phone rang. She announced that it was Emily calling.

"Hey, Lady," she said, answering her phone, restrained excitement in her voice. Cosmo could hear Emily say hello to his sister. She had a distinctive voice, part sexy and scratchy, and part kind and innocent. Silvia's phone volume was turned loud enough for him to hear everything.

"Hey, Silvia," Emily said. "Where are you?"

"We're at the start of our trip. In Maryland. We'll be there within the week." She was so sure they'd be there within the week. She should have said they'd be there within the week, accounting for a host of mishaps that could happen along the way. But that wasn't her style.

"Don't forget to call as you get closer," Emily said. "I'm so excited to see you!"

The drive through Maryland continued on with rolling hills and trees and soon they were on to the next state. As Cosmo stared at the Virginia welcome sign, he thought they were making great time, but then he looked at the clock and noticed it was half-past three in the afternoon.

"Do we have to be in Memphis tonight?" Cosmo asked.

"Well, yeah," Silvia said, her head not swaying from watching the road. "It's a free place to stay."

"We're going to get there really late. I hope your friend doesn't care."

"Oh no, Clay won't care. He's a night owl."

Cosmo sunk down in his seat and closed his eyes. He thought he'd try to take a nap, and just as he began to doze off, Silvia turned on some music. It wasn't loud or abrasive music, but it was enough to jar him out of his potential nap.

"I was just dozing off, Silv," he said, annoyed.

"I'm sorry," she said. "I was starting to get highway hypnosis."

He shook his head, slanted his lips, and rolled his eyes. Just as he was being annoyed at his little sister, who was always sorry, who was always coming up with some new symptom or some reason to change the environment in some way, it happened. A Mack truck swerved into their lane, forcing Silvia to go off the road and into the grass-filled partition. Time stopped. Cosmo felt as if he wasn't there, as if he slipped away from his body and was watching the whole thing from above. They both sat there, sharing the same feelings of shock, relief, and confusion. It happened before he knew it was happening, so fast and bizarre that he couldn't piece it together in his mind.

"Jesus fucking Christ!" Silvia said. She rambled on about how she couldn't believe what had happened, how truck drivers drove for too long of a time, and how they took too many amphetamines to keep going. Cosmo heard her as if she was talking to him from a distance. Her voice sounded farther and farther away until it faded completely, and Cosmo didn't hear anything. Not even the voice in his head. He wasn't in an out-of-body place of fading sound for too long, as the sound of a police siren crashed into his world. He was glad his sister was able to talk to the officer. She didn't seem nearly as shaken as he was. Maybe she'd had a similar experience with all her time on the road. Otherwise, she wouldn't have been able to react so well.

"You all right?" the cop asked.

"Just barely," Silvia said, who was surprising Cosmo more and more each second by her composure. She was even getting out her license for the cop.

"These truck drivers drive too long," the cop said, looking at her license. He went on about how he had seen it from a distance and was impressed with how well Silvia reacted.

"Thank you," she said, opening the glove compartment, undoubtedly to get out her registration. The officer was barely interested in seeing her license and seemed less interested in seeing her registration. He was more interested in talking about the size of the truck, which apparently was an eighteen-wheeler, and how lucky both of them were that she reacted so well. "I hate to say it, but you're lucky to be alive." He poked his potato-shaped head in and looked Cosmo right in the eye, almost as if he was warning him about something.

Cosmo nodded his head in agreement and expressed his gratitude to the cop, who suggested they pull over at the next rest stop and take a break from the road. But Silvia said she was fine to keep driving, thanked the cop, and was on her way. She talked continuously about the incident as she drove and about how something like that had happened before to her, but she wasn't driving at the time. She talked on and on, her words still blurring together in Cosmo's head. He was still not sure of what had just happened. And now he felt nauseous, which he attributed to the combination of their near-fatal accident and Frank's frittata. He needed to get out of the car, and he needed to now.

"Silvia, please pull over at the next stop," he said.

"We're never going to make it if we keep pulling over," she said. But the tone of her voice didn't have any fight in it, as if her understanding his wanting to stop outweighed her urgency to make it to Memphis that night.

"So fucking what if we don't make it," he said. "I feel like I'm going to throw up. We almost died, for Christ's sake. I'll pay for a motel tonight if we can't make it to Memphis."

"It's not that," she said. "It's just that I'd planned to make it there tonight."

"Well, sometimes you have to alter your plans," he said. "Aren't you always talking about how adaptable you are?"

"Yeah, all right," she said reluctantly. She got in the exit lane and pulled off at a rest stop that was nothing more than a bathroom facility. Seconds after Cosmo's feet reached the ground, the uneasiness in his stomach started to fade. He walked over to a picnic table that was only a few feet away from the car, sat down, and looked up at the surrounding trees. Their golden leaves flickered in the fading sunlight. As he looked at the trees, he felt nothing but gratitude. He was grateful his nausea went away, grateful that he could see the fall-colored trees, and grateful that his little sister was by his side. Most of all, he was grateful to be alive.

Chapter 4

A s Cosmo looked out the car window, he felt as if he was seeing the world for the first time in his life. And in some ways, he was. The Blue Ridge Mountains were stunning. Layers of mountains with one blending into the next, clouds settling on the tops of them. The faraway mountains were so faded by the late afternoon light cast upon them that they were almost white. As the sun was setting, strips of orange and pink light spread across the sky.

As soon as the sun went down, they found a motel. It was a cheap motel, but it was comfortable. Still, Cosmo couldn't get to sleep. Each time he drifted off, he got visions of them flying off the road. After a couple of hours, he got up and tried to read to get his mind off the event of the day. But it was no use. The pictures in his mind were too strong. Silvia woke up in the middle of the night to use the bathroom, and upon seeing that her brother was still awake, said she'd make him some chamomile tea. She used the coffee maker in the room to warm up some water and put two, not one, tea bags in a cup. She had a variety of herbal tea bags stashed in her backpack. He hadn't realized until that moment how prepared his sister always was for everything. She carried food, water, and tea with her everywhere. Soon after drinking the tea, he was off to sleep.

He only slept five hours but woke feeling refreshed. He wondered how he could feel refreshed after sleeping for such a short time, and then he remembered he and Silvia had almost died the day before. He reasoned the gratitude he felt for being alive made him happy, and that the happiness gave him energy. In addition to feeling energized, he was excited to get on the road and see a part of the world he had never seen. He was even tempted to wake his sister, but he knew how she relished her sleep. She never liked to be awakened. He could still see Donna trying to pull a younger Silvia from her bed in the morning before school, her little arms holding on tight to the bedposts.

So instead of waking his sister, he took a shower and made some coffee. He opened the drapes to look out as he drank his coffee, and the light must have wakened Silvia. He looked over at her to see her stretching her arms over her head and yawning contentedly like she had a good night's sleep. With her being so well rested, Cosmo thought, maybe she'd be able to do most of the driving so he could look out of the window at the scenery.

"Hey, do you mind doing most of the driving today?" Cosmo asked her as soon as she opened her eyes. "I didn't sleep so great."

"No problem," she said, hopping out of bed.

The flora of Tennessee was more lush and green than he could have ever imagined. Some of the greenery was changing into fall colors, and some of the fall colors were in full bloom. Behind the leaf-filled trees were the

Great Smoky Mountains, which were just as magnificent as the previous mountain range.

The slowness of the south came through to Cosmo in a way that seemed to permeate his skin. Like the rate of his blood passing through his veins had slowed. Even through the fast moving automobile in which they were encapsulated, he could feel the slowness of the place. In the rest stops, he noticed how people talked and moved slower than they did in the Northeast. He attributed the increased slowness to the heaviness of the southern air. It made sense that the moist, wet, warm air should slow everything down.

He hadn't spent any time in the South, except for passing through on their family trip to Florida. He didn't consider Florida as being part of the South. When he thought of the South, he thought of twangy accents, corn dogs, and a place with a fierce devotion to its tradition; a place with a haunted past and ghost-filled swamps. He was now experiencing it in a different light, seeing its lush beauty and feeling its stuck-in-time slowness. He liked it.

They hadn't stopped to get any food all day. Silvia had been eating from her grocery bag of food, and Cosmo forgot to eat, as he was too engulfed in seeing the scenes. He felt a great, gaping hole in his stomach as it cried out for food. He wanted to stop and eat, but he also wanted to wait for Memphis in hopes of getting some of their famous barbeque.

"Do you have anything in that bag I might like?" Cosmo asked Silvia.

"Oh yeah," she said right away. "There are some blue corn chips in a big plastic bag inside the black canvas bag."

Cosmo had never eaten blue corn chips or even heard of them. He thought a lot of the food Silvia ate was nonsense, but after eating only a few of the chips, he decided they were great. He wondered why he hadn't stumbled upon them sooner. As he munched the chips, thinking about how great they were, he considered how small his world had become. His fascination at a new type of snack food was telling of his shrinking universe. The smallness of his world didn't come from the fact that he led a sheltered existence. It came from the sameness in his life. The way he ate the same food, read the same kind of books, went to the same shops, did the same activities, listened to the same music, walked the same way to work, talked to the same people, watched the same movies, and thought the same thoughts. He hadn't had a new idea since college.

"We're almost there," Silvia said, taking Cosmo out of his blue corn chip contemplation. "I'm going to call Clay." She took her phone out of her backpack and in a few seconds was speaking to her friend.

"Hey, Clay," she said with excitement. "We're almost there!" Cosmo could hear her friend talking through the phone with a nice-sounding, gentle voice. He imagined all her friends were nice, gentle, flighty, and poor like she was. After they wrapped up their plans, she said she'd drive because it was easier than telling Cosmo the directions Clay had given her.

"Okay," Cosmo said. "But I need to eat something, and as long as we're in Memphis, I'm eating barbeque."

"All right," Silvia said, who didn't sound so happy about the idea of barbeque. "Maybe we can find a place that has barbequed tofu." Cosmo could tell she was joking by a mild laughter in her voice.

The place they found didn't have barbequed tofu, but it did have macaroni and cheese and collard greens for Silvia, and she seemed to love the food she ordered. Cosmo was sure, though, that she couldn't have loved her food as much as he loved his barbeque. He was grateful Silvia didn't make him feel like a murderer as he sat with a big plate of ribs before him. He was so into his food that for the first time in his trip, he barely took notice of the atmosphere. There wasn't much of an atmosphere in this place though. It was a big, square room with fake wood paneled walls, square plastic tables, and mismatched chairs. All of the other people inside looked like they were there for one thing—the food.

As Cosmo chewed, his temples rubbed against his hat and he felt tempted to take it off. Something in him wouldn't let him take the hat off. Was it the big-ness of his hair that he didn't want to show the world? And if so, why? He wasn't at all self-conscious. Maybe it was because his hair made the rest of him stand out and with his hair, he couldn't hide. He couldn't be invisible.

It was almost eight when they had finished dinner, at which time they headed straight over to Clay's. He lived in a colorful district filled with old, brick buildings that looked as if they had been standing solid through several generations. Presently, the buildings housed restaurants, condos, and shops, although they looked as if they had been used as warehouses many years ago. The area could have even been an industrial center at one time—at a time when things were actually made in this country. Cosmo imagined that it had been deserted for decades and had only been revived in recent years.

Clay was waiting for them underneath a blue and white marquee sign. He had reddish hair pulled back in a ponytail and a smile that stretched from one side of his face to the other. He didn't look at all how Cosmo pictured him. Silvia mentioned that he was a blues musician, so Cosmo had pictured someone who looked like Muddy Waters or B.B. King. He didn't picture a young white guy with red hair. Still, he was dressed like a blues guy might be dressed in suspenders, rolled up jeans, and work boots.

"Hey, Clay," Silvia said, giving Clay a platonic hug. "This is my brother, Cosmo." The two shook hands.

"Nice to meet you," Clay said in a deep, but playful voice.

"You guys hungry or did you eat already?" Clay asked as they walked down the street.

"We ate," Silvia said. "But we didn't have dessert." As she said this, they happened to be passing by a place that had a red awning with the word 'cheesecake' on it.

"You all like cheesecake, right?" Clay asked, stopping in front of the place.

"Who doesn't?" Cosmo said, and with that, they all walked in and had a seat at a small table in the window.

━━

"How did you guys meet?" Cosmo asked Silvia and Clay as he put a forkful of cheesecake in his mouth.

"We worked in a health food store together. That's how we met," Silvia said as she scraped her fork against her plate, gathering remnants of graham cracker crust. "We used to go out," she added, smirking. Cosmo looked over at Clay to see him smiling into the air.

"But now we're just friends," Clay said, continuing from where Silvia left off. Cosmo wasn't interested in delving into his little sister's romantic life and was relieved when she changed the subject.

"I quit after only a couple months, but Clay stayed," she said.

"You still in touch with anybody else from work?" Clay asked, sitting back in his chair.

"Just Kristen," Silvia said, taking a sip from her tea. "I lost touch with Mike."

"Oh yeah, Mike," Clay said, grinning and raising his eyebrows.

"Mike was a kleptomaniac," Silvia said to Cosmo. "They caught him stealing a crate of falafel mix."

"Wow," Cosmo said. "What a weird thing to steal. Couldn't he have gone for something more expensive and less obvious? I don't know, maybe a bottle of lavender oil or something." They all shared a laugh at poor Mike's expense and Silvia explained that kleptomaniacs want to be caught and that this desire was all a part of the disease. She really had it all figured out. Out of what appeared to be courtesy, Clay paid attention to her analysis.

"So what brought you to Philly, and what drove you away?" Cosmo asked Clay.

"Music," Clay said, as if music was all there was in his life. Cosmo raised his eyebrows to Clay as if to say, "Go on" and so Clay did go on. He talked about how he started playing guitar when he was a boy. He learned from his dad, who learned from his dad, who probably also learned from his dad. He talked about how he joined his first band in high school and how they played a mixture of post punk and sixties psychedelic. He joined with another band after high school, and this was the band with whom he moved to Philadelphia. When they broke up, all the members scattered around the country. He wanted to move some place where he could study the blues. Cosmo assumed he was in school.

"There's a good music school around here?" asked Cosmo.

"I'm not really part of a school," Clay said. "I do have a teacher though, and he's great." He took a bite of his cheesecake and asked Cosmo, "What about you? What do you study?" He asked this question as if he assumed that Cosmo was a student of something.

"I dropped out of college a while ago," Cosmo said, putting his head down.

"That doesn't mean anything," Clay said. "You don't have to be a student to be studying something." Cosmo had never considered that truth until now.

"I studied astronomy in college," Cosmo said, picking his head up, feeling a bit of pride.

"Yikes! You must be smart," Clay said. "Science always goes right over my head." He swept his hand across his head from front to back.

Cosmo was used to getting this response when he told someone what he studied in college. He hadn't told anyone in a long time, and almost forgot how good it felt to get that sort of response. He was modest though and brushed away Clay's comment with a gesture, waving his hand and smirking as if to say that he wasn't a genius by any means. But Silvia wouldn't let him.

"He's the brains of the family," she said.

"You do a lot of star gazing, huh?" Clay said.

"Not so much lately," Cosmo said. He couldn't re-member the last time he gazed at the stars with his telescope. It must have been at least over five years ago. Maybe six.

—◂—

After cheesecake, they headed over to Clay's apartment, which was only a couple of blocks walk. It was above a small, corner grocery store and was up two long flights of steps. Inside, it was a big, cavernous space with worn hardwood floors, very large rectangular windows, and high ceilings. It was dingy and messy, and it felt familiar and comfortable to Cosmo because it was so much like his own apartment. A brown worn couch sat in the center of the room. It faced windows that revealed a view of the building across the alleyway. Music filled the room: A stereo with a record player and speakers as big as Silvia, rows of vinyl albums stacked up against the walls, two acoustic guitars and one electric, harmonicas scattered on tables, and a black, hard music case sized to fit a saxophone. Cosmo could play the guitar and the violin, but he couldn't remember the last time he played either. An electric guitar sat in his apartment collecting dust—he hadn't picked it up for at least two years. His violin was at Frank's house, which meant that he hadn't touched it since he left his dad's house at age eighteen.

He took violin lessons as a boy. His boyhood violin teacher was the first person to tell him about his perfect pitch. His name was Mr. Porcelli, and he could still see the little, mustached, bow tie wearing man now, saying to Frank in his broken English voice, "Ah the boy has perfect pitch. What a gift." Cosmo remembered seeing something in Frank's face that didn't look like the expression of a proud parent. It was more of a look of envy mixed with confusion, probably from wondering from whom Cosmo had inherited his musical gift. But Frank was, after all, the person who got him started with music lessons. He could be so enigmatic.

Cosmo wondered why he stopped playing the violin. He loved playing the violin. He taught himself to play the guitar once he moved away from his home in New Jersey, and he loved playing that too. He could play for hours, with hours feeling like mere minutes. He looked over at a large acoustic guitar in the corner of the room and had an urge to start playing it. Clay must have noticed him staring at the guitar.

"You play guitar?" Clay asked him.

"Not for a while," Cosmo said, discouraged.

"Well, be my guest if you want to," Clay said.

Cosmo took him up on the offer. He grabbed the guitar and sat down on the couch. All of his calluses were long gone, and he was additionally challenged by the fact that the guitar had thick steel strings. But his urge to play was so strong that he didn't care about what little bit of pain he'd feel in his fingers.

"Play a Beatles song, and I'll sing," Silvia said, smiling and standing as if she was ready to do a cheer.

"How do you know I can play any Beatles songs?" Cosmo asked Silvia.

"Because you played them for me when I came to visit you in Philly when I was in high school. Remember?" He didn't remember. Maybe his memory was going, and if it was, he could only assume that his memory for making chord shapes was gone. But the second his fingers touched the strings, it all came back to him, as if his fingers had a memory of their own. He started to play *Hey Jude* and Silvia joined in singing and Clay grabbed another guitar and played along. It was like a musical where all the cast members extemporaneously joined in song. It was a thing of beauty.

Afterward, Cosmo asked Clay to play some blues. As Clay played, his face filled with light, growing brighter and brighter as he played on. Cosmo remembered seeing the same kind of light in his own face at one time. Now when he looked in the mirror, he saw a dull, lifeless face looking back. He wished he could get that light back in his face. He knew he couldn't get that light back by playing the blues. That wasn't his passion. His passion was learning and when he stopped learning, a part of him died, or at least, went to sleep. Maybe now, it was waking up.

———

When Cosmo was awakened by Silvia at eight in the morning, he wished he could go back to sleep but knew that they needed to get on the road. He slept on an old, worn futon that Clay had rolled out for him, and calculated in his head that he had only slept about five hours. Another night of deprived sleep. He didn't regret staying up late though because his time spent playing the guitar and talking with Clay was well worth any amount of lost sleep.

"I made you a cup of coffee," Silvia said as she placed a cup down on a table near where Cosmo slept. After she placed the cup down, she went back into the kitchen. She was in her morning rush mode.

Cosmo assumed that Clay was still sleeping, as he stayed awake even after Cosmo had gone to sleep. But he was wrong. Clay popped in the room looking half-asleep with mop hair and the same clothes he had on last night. Still, he didn't seem tired or grumpy; rather, he seemed energized. Cosmo didn't notice the way he walked the previous night, but now he saw his walk was somewhat like Vince's walk. He moved with the top of his body tilted forward, as if there were urgency about getting wherever he was going. His way of walking didn't seem to be out of nervousness or anxiety, but out of enthusiasm and a desire to cram all the learning and living he could into each day.

"Hey, Cosmo," Clay said. "Hungry? I got donuts in the kitchen."

"Oh, thanks a lot," Cosmo said, sitting up. "Don't mind if I do."

Cosmo followed Clay into the kitchen where Silvia was talking to a young man who was apparently one of

Clay's roommates. He was stout man with a big smile and an even bigger head of afro hair. Cosmo intended to introduce himself to Clay's roommate but his sister intercepted him.

"James, this is my brother," she said as she poured some coffee into a cup.

"Hey," Cosmo said to James. "Nice to meet you."

"You too," James said.

"James works at the same restaurant as Clay," Silvia told her brother.

"Cool," Cosmo said, sipping from his coffee that was badly in need of some cream.

"What kind of restaurant is it?" Cosmo asked, glancing around for cream.

"It's yuppie southern," James said, who must have noticed Cosmo's searching eyes. "You need something?"

"Yeah," Cosmo said. "Cream or milk."

"Oh, here," Silvia said, handing him a container of half-and-half that was hiding behind her.

"Thanks," Cosmo said to Silvia. He then turned to James and said, "What's southern yuppie? Like grits with truffle oil?"

"Yeah," James said through a laugh. "That's it."

Just as Cosmo grabbed one of the donuts Clay had put out on a dish, he saw Silvia look at the clock on the wall. He knew they had to be on their way, so Cosmo quickly shoved the donut in his mouth and gulped down his coffee. The donut was stale, so he wouldn't have enjoyed it anymore if he took his time eating it.

"We have to get going," Silvia said, looking at Clay with a fake frown on her face.

"Wait," Clay said running out of the room. "I got something for you."

He came back in the room in a flash with a couple of CDs in his hand. "I burned you these," he said, giving the CDs to Silvia. "I was afraid you wouldn't have any Dylan for the road."

"I got *Highway 61 Revisited*," Silvia said who looked back at her friend as if she took offense to his comment.

"You need more than one Dylan CD for your trip," he said seriously. "That's all you should be listening to for the whole trip."

"What about Neil Young?" Silvia asked, a chuckle in her voice.

But Clay wasn't taking this question with any sort of humor. He looked up at the ceiling as if contemplating her question with the utmost seriousness. "Yeah, Neil Young might be all right."

And with that they said their goodbyes and were on their way.

—▬—

As soon as they got in the car, Cosmo put in the Dylan CD that Clay had made for Silvia. Cosmo remembered hearing him as a child, as he was one of Donna's favorites. At the time, he thought his music was boring and that his voice was whiny. But now as he listened to it, he heard something completely different. Almost as if he were hearing Dylan for the first time. He heard the poetry in his lyrics, the subtle strength in his voice, the beauty, hardship, desolation, and story that was the American road.

Chapter 5

The bridge over the Mississippi River was made of mint green arches that rose and fell like a great mountain built by human hands. The river looked both calm and majestic at the same time. Cosmo was sorry that he was the current driver, which made it impossible for him to stare at the great body of water as much as he would have liked, but he was grateful for having seen it at all. He wished his sister wasn't so rushed to get to the other side of the country, and that they could go on a cruise on the river. He wished he could have spent more time at Clay's. He wished they could have driven through Tennessee at a leisurely pace so he could enjoy and absorb the flora and fauna that he'd most probably never see again. She drove with a lead foot, and when he tried to drive any slower than seventy-five miles per hour, she told him to speed up.

"Why is there such a rush to get to Portland?" he asked her, not turning away from the steering wheel.

"I have a lot to do once I get to Portland," she said. "I have to find a place to live and get a job and get settled."

"But what does getting there in a hurry have to do with any of that stuff?" he said. "I mean, it's not like all the jobs and all the places to live are going to go away by a certain time. Besides, I thought you said you were moving in with your friend."

"Well, I'm not absolutely sure I can move in with Emily. And I feel anxious to get there so I can start setting myself up. It's not easy to do all that stuff." Her tone of voice became progressively defensive as she spoke. Cosmo still couldn't understand his sister's need for rushing, and he knew he never would understand it because it wasn't a genuine need. It was some contrived excuse to continue rushing through her life.

"I feel like we're on the run from one of Dad's crazy rampages or something," Cosmo said. "You remember them, right?" He was sure that she remembered them, probably only all too well.

"Yeah," she said, staring out the window. "All I ever wanted was for Mom to keep driving. I didn't want to stop at a motel in Jersey. I wished that she could just drive and drive and drive until we made it to the other side of this big fat country."

Maybe she was still running away from one of Frank's rampages. From the loud, mad space that their house would become from time to time. Cosmo searched himself for something to say to let her know that there was no longer any need to run, but his mind was blank. He thought that he might have more to say if he could relate to what she was saying, but he couldn't. He hated the times that they had to leave the house in a panic, and when they did, he wanted Donna to stop at the very first place they could find. He never wanted her to keep driving. He felt relieved once they returned home the next day to find a remorseful, guilty father who would be good until his next upheaval.

"Didn't you like it when we could all go back home the next day and Dad felt like really awful and he was nice to us for a while?"

"I hated going back home," she said decisively.

"Well those days are long gone. You can stop running." He regretted these words as soon as his words hit the air. He knew the word 'running' would make her defensive and he was right.

"I'm not running," she said as if she were trying to convince herself of this fact.

"I meant to say rushing. You can stop rushing."

Silvia didn't say anything for a few seconds and the brief silence led Cosmo to believe that he had gotten through to her on some level. But he knew that this was not the case when she said, "I think we should stop to get gas. We're almost on empty."

The ride through Arkansas was filled with gentle hills rolling into one another, and with fall-colored trees that lived in the spaces in between the hills. In the distance, Cosmo could see the Ozark Mountains. He spotted a pull-off up ahead and asked Silvia to stop.

"Do we have to?" she whined.

"Please," he said. "Just for a minute."

From the pull-out, Cosmo could see the many layers of mountains. The layer furthest from his view melded with the sky, and the demarcation between the horizon and the mountains was almost indistinguishable. The next layer showed green and orange colors, with yellow poking through here and there. He could see individual trees and open spaces in the mountains closest to his view. As he looked at the mountains, he noticed how his eyes didn't burn as they usually did, despite having a short night's sleep. He then remembered that the past two days had been computer-free days. Yesterday, he didn't even turn on his phone. It felt good to see the world with refreshed eyes.

"Do your eyes ever burn?" he asked Silvia.

"Well yeah," she said, seemingly baffled by his question. "When I haven't slept enough. Why do you ask?"

"Because today is the first day in years that mine haven't burned," he said, scratching his head. "I guess I just got used to feeling them burn all the time."

"Well if I was looking at a computer screen twenty-four seven, I'm sure mine would burn all the time too."

"Yeah," he said, gazing at the mountains.

"Do you want to go back to that burning eye job?"

"What else would I do? I can't imagine anything else."

"I don't believe that. I think you haven't allowed yourself to imagine anything else. Anything different. Anything new."

～

Around midway through Oklahoma, the scenery changed, becoming more flat and dull and open than the previous states. Less trees, more wide-open prairies. Cosmo contemplated how this place had been devastated by natural catastrophes over and over again, and he even felt the remnants of struggle and hardship lingering in the air. And yet there was a kind of beauty in the starkness. The light in the sky was starting to fade as early evening approached, and his stomach cried out for food. He realized he had only eaten snack food all day and now he wanted something real.

"Hey, I want to stop to eat next place we see," he said to Silvia, who was driving.

"All right," she said. "But the next place is probably going to be a truck stop."

Eating at a truck stop would be a first for Cosmo. He liked the idea of it, and he was glad that his sister was correct in her prediction. They pulled into a place with a very tall sign that said *Petro.* The building itself was a big, plain, flat square and it contained restrooms, a restaurant, and a convenience store. Outside the building, there were two places for gas—one for cars and one for trucks. The one for trucks had tall pumps—tall enough for giants.

Cosmo glanced around at the truck stop with interest and curiosity. He looked at Silvia, who seemed completely disinterested in their surroundings. He wondered if it was because she had seen all this before or if it was because she was in such a rush to get to Portland. He didn't know whether to feel envious that she had seen so much in her short life, or to feel sorry for her because she hadn't really seen all the stuff she saw. He decided to go with the latter. She was a painter and a great one too. How could she be a painter and not see the world around her? She was always into her surroundings as a girl. They all took a day trip to Philly one cold winter day, and all she had wanted to do was to stare at the tops of the buildings. When had that part of her faded out?

The restaurant inside of the truck stop reminded Cosmo of a more open and much less charming version of an east coast diner. This place was pure functionality, nothing frivolous such as mini jukeboxes at the tables. Just a big, box-shaped space with fake wooden tables scattered throughout it and some beige vinyl booths lining the walls. A lady in an apron greeted them. She was slumped over so badly that her face looked almost straight down at the floor. She lifted her head up slightly to ask if a booth was all right, and this motion seemed to require great effort. Her face was tired and worn, almost as if she was sleeping with her eyes open. She seated them and said she'd be right back to take their order.

They sat at a booth that was on the side of the room and had a window that looked out to the tall gas pumps for trucks. They got suspicious glares from some of the other customers, who mostly appeared to be truck drivers. They were easy to spot because their bodies looked as if they had been formed from several years of driving trucks, and they stood all hunched over and forward leaning. Cosmo and his sister stood out with their youthful looks, dark features, and Silvia's hip clothes. All of the other customers also looked to be a part of the place, like it was a kind of home for them, and now two uninvited guests had popped in for dinner.

Cosmo couldn't recall ever feeling like an outsider. He didn't mind the feeling. He actually liked it because it made him feel unique. In Philadelphia, he always blended in so well with all the people around him that it was easy to forget who he was. Here, he couldn't forget that he was Cosmo Greco, part geek, part scientist, part slacker; an east-coast Italian-American, or as the people here might say, 'eye-talian-American.'

He was even tempted to ask the waitress about what kind of salad dressing they had, so that he might have an opportunity to see if she'd say 'eye-talian.' He didn't, but he was happy that Silvia did, and sure enough, the poor old thing did mispronounce the word exactly as he thought she would. He kept himself from laughing, but it wasn't easy, because he saw Silvia make a smile of restrained laughter as soon as the waitress said the word. She then asked the waitress about the soup. Maybe his little sister was turning into their mom, who always had a long list of questions for the wait staff.

"Is there any chicken broth in the soup?" Silvia asked, sitting up straight, eyes alert. "Because I'm vegetarian."

The waitress looked disinterested in Silvia's dietary requirements, and Cosmo felt sorry for the lady, who said that she didn't know if the soup was made with chicken broth. She offered to go back in the kitchen to ask the cooks. Cosmo was greatly relieved that Silvia didn't have her go back and ask the cooks in the kitchen, and that she decided upon a grilled cheese sandwich.

"And what'll you have, sir?" she said, looking at Cosmo. He couldn't remember the last time someone addressed him as 'sir' and for a second, he didn't know if she was talking to him or to someone else.

"I'll have a cheeseburger and fries," he said, looking at Silvia as though he was expecting her to make a comment about his choice of entree. She didn't say anything, but her face told him enough about her feelings on his poor choice. So when the waitress left the table, Cosmo responded to Silvia's stare.

"I saw your little look, Silv."

"What look?" she said, smirking.

"Not everybody wants to live on rice and beans. And hey, maybe I would've got a tofu burger if it was an option, but I don't think we'll be finding any such thing in these here parts." He put on a southern accent.

"Sorry," she said half-laughing. Her ability to say 'sorry' always impressed Cosmo. She was an anomaly in the Greco family in that way. He wished he had some of that same ability, but he had none. Maybe if he were more capable of apologizing, he and Angie would talk to each other on a somewhat regular basis, or at least more than once every six years. He thought his change of heart towards Angie had something to do with nearly being killed a couple of days ago. Resenting his sister had been another way he had wasted the time he had on this planet.

Silvia tried to bring the two together when she planned a family gathering for Vince's high school graduation last year. And she did succeed in bringing them together in the same room, but Cosmo couldn't bring himself to talk to Angie any more than just greeting her. He wished he could go back in time and go to the party all over again. Silvia was the only family member who was capable of arranging such a family gathering, and now with her moving to Portland, there was no hope of having another such occasion.

He looked over at her dissecting her cheese sandwich, probably to inspect it for any signs of meat. He almost wished that he'd had the time and energy to concern himself with such nonsense. But as much as she worried about nonsense, she didn't sit around and regret things like he was doing right now. She didn't regret. She didn't go backward. She was too busy plotting and planning for the future. And now, it appeared as though Cosmo and Emily were a part of her future plans.

"I think you should meet Emily," she said taking a bite of her sandwich. "I think you would be great together."

"Why's that?" Cosmo said as he shoved some fries in his mouth. He didn't sound too enthused.

"Because you guys are so much alike. Emily's a girl geek. She's a gamer. She's really smart. She's such a geek that she can probably recite lines from Monty Python. I think she even listens to the same music as you. Oh, and she's pretty."

Cosmo didn't bother responding, but not because he thought Silvia's comment didn't warrant a response. He didn't say anything because the sudden sick, empty feeling in his stomach consumed him. He already liked the little bit that he knew of Emily from her voice on the phone, and now Silvia was giving him a bunch of other reasons to like her. What if he met her and he really liked her? What then? He'd move to Portland and get a barista job, and maybe he'd become one of those poor, happy hipsters he liked to make fun of. Maybe he shouldn't even go all the way to Portland. Maybe he should turn back early. He could get his sister through the scarier part of the country, and leave her on her own in California. He had never been in California but imagined it to be safer than all the states leading up to there. Vince's presence in the state only added to Cosmo's image of this place as a safe haven for Silvia.

As he imagined going back early, the sickness in his stomach lessened, and he was able to eat the rest of his food. He was also happy that Silvia didn't persist in swaying him to get excited about meeting her friend. She knew him well enough to know what he was thinking, and she was smart enough to know when to lay off. So instead of saying anything more, she left for the restroom, leaving Cosmo a chance to check his email on his phone.

He hadn't checked his email in over forty-eight hours and couldn't remember the last time he went so long without checking it. Maybe never. It felt good to be away from his email, not checking it compulsively out of sheer boredom. He had been living so much life the past two days that he hadn't even thought of checking it. There were over fifty messages in his inbox, ninety percent of which were junk. A few days ago, he probably wouldn't have seen them as junk. Something about nearly dying had changed his perception of the importance of such things. There was one message that wasn't junk though, and that was his credit card bill. He had forgotten about the money thing since he had been on the road. What a rude awakening to see a bill for over one thousand dollars. What games and gadgets had he purchased to color in his days? He couldn't even remember now. But he knew he had spent all the money that was on this bill, and now he stared at it as if he was somehow disconnected from it. Once again, he thought of returning home early and going back to a job where he could make money and pay bills. And once again the thought of going home brought relief and comfort to him.

Just as he was planning his escape from the trip, two women walked by him and sat in the adjoining booth.

One of the women was bald. Her face was ashen, worn, and sunken-in, but her eyes shone like she knew some sacred truth, or as if she had seen something that everyone around her missed. The woman with her had a look of forced strength in her face that drooped down as if heavy with sadness.

Cosmo was curious about the two women, and he had started forming a story about them in his mind. The bald one had obviously undergone chemotherapy, and therefore had cancer. The other woman appeared to be a close friend and seemed sadder than the woman with cancer. He was looking forward to eavesdropping on their conversation without any interruptions from Silvia, but she had just returned to the table with a new menu in hand, searching for something else with which to bother the waitress.

"I want something sweet now," she said as soon as she sat down. "Oh, here comes the waitress." She rubbed her hands together, smiling.

"What kind of milkshakes do you have?" Silvia asked the waitress, who looked like she may have aged since their arrival into the place.

"Ah," said the waitress, as if she was unsure of the answer to this question. "I guess we can make you any flavor of ice cream you want. Chocolate, vanilla."

"Okay, I'll get chocolate." Silvia said this as if she expected the waitress to get excited about her selection, but that wasn't the case at all. She simply said "okay" and slumped away toward the kitchen.

"Why didn't you get something too?" Silvia asked, and then without giving Cosmo a chance to respond, she said. "You can't have any of mine."

Cosmo didn't bother responding. He just smiled and nodded his head. Silvia ignored his response and stood up suddenly as if she had something important to do. "I want to ask her if she has any malt," she said. "I love malted milkshakes." As she ran off to look for the waitress, Cosmo heard the sound of a lady crying. It was one of the ladies in the booth next to them. He then heard the other woman's attempt at consolation: "Please don't cry, Maggie. I'm not crying. I'm not sad. And I don't feel like I was ripped off either. I had a wonderful life. And it doesn't matter how long you get here. All that matters is what you do with the time you have." This must have been the great secret that showed in her eyes. These wise words reverberated inside Cosmo as all thoughts about credit card bills, moving back to Philadelphia, and meeting Emily vanished from his mind. And as he sat back in his seat, he felt so full and warm and light inside, as if the light of the wise woman had spread to him.

Just then, Silvia came back to the table, smiling big and bright. "They have malt!"

Cosmo smiled back at her. She reminded him of Frank, who also turned into a big kid at the promise of ice cream. As the waitress approached the table, Silvia looked as if she wanted to jump out of her skin. The waitress held a milkshake topped with whipped cream in a glass that looked too big for little Silvia. As she put the glass down on the table, Cosmo heard the ladies beside him comment on the milkshake. "Oh, that looks delicious," said the bald lady in a more playful voice than the one she spoke in previously. "We better get a couple of those ourselves."

When they got back to the car, the sky had turned dark, and the air felt clean and dry. Between the feeling in the air, the coffee he'd had with dinner, and most of all, the words he was so fortunate to hear from the angelic woman in the restaurant, he felt filled with energy, and he told Silvia he would drive. He drove until they almost reached the Texas border, and then they started looking for motels.

"There's a sign for one, Cos," Silvia said, pointing to a sign on the side of the road. "I think it's a cheap one too. Let's take the exit."

Cosmo followed along with his sister's wishes, although he felt as if he could have kept driving. In fact, he felt as if he could drive all through the night. He wanted to see as much of the countryside as he could though, and he knew he needed the light of day to see it. He took the exit and followed the motel sign, turning right onto a narrow, unlit road. After driving only a few feet, he could see some lights in the distance, and as he got closer to the source of lights, he saw a gas station, a Denny's, and a motel. The phrase one-horse town came into his head, but instead of feeling down on the place, he felt eager to see more of it in the morning light.

As he pulled into the driveway of the motel, he felt that same feeling of the clutch slipping. He was about to tell Silvia about it when they neared a sign just outside the motel that said read: "CLEAN ROOMS RUN BY AMERICANS."

"That's too weird," Silvia said, referring to the sign. "Let's go somewhere else."

"What if there's nothing else?" Cosmo said, mildly curious to see the inside of the place, given its bizarre sign.

"Well then, I'll sleep in the car," she said, leaning back in her seat.

So he drove on down the road, and within a few minutes, a railroad-style motel came into view. No weird sign on the outside of the place, and on the inside, an elderly man in a white button down shirt, who appeared to be from the fifties, greeted them. He wore a pair of plastic-frame glasses with such thick lenses that Cosmo could barely see his eyes. He appeared to be delighted to have some customers, as if he hadn't had any all day. The lobby was a small room with a bright red carpet and dark brown paneled walls decorated with paintings of cowboys.

Their room didn't look much different than the lobby minus the bright red carpeting. There was a kind of charm in the old room they were given; it had two twin sized beds, and old furniture, all of which looked as though it had been bought at a garage sale. It was clean though, and the toilet in the bathroom even had a seal wrapped across the top of it to indicate that it had just been cleaned. There was a television in the center of the room, but Cosmo had no interest in turning it on. Silvia was lounging on one of the beds reading a beaten up copy of *Siddartha*. Cosmo had brought a bunch of books, but he didn't feel like reading. He couldn't stop thinking about the lady from the truck stop, and he wanted to talk about her, even if it meant he had to interrupt his sister's reading.

"Did you catch any of the conversation of the ladies sitting next to us?" He knew she hadn't caught any of this conversation, but he needed some way to open up the discussion.

"No," she said without looking up from her book. Cosmo waited a few seconds for her to ask a follow-up question, but nothing came from her lips.

"Well, I can't stop thinking about it," he said, gazing out of the window. He saw his sister look up from her book out of the corner of his eye.

"Really," she said in a curious voice. "Why?"

"Because of what they were talking about."

"What was that?"

"Well, the one lady had cancer, apparently, and it sounded as if the doctor had given her a short amount of time to live. The other lady started crying, and then the one with cancer said something...." He turned and looked at his sister, who was now giving him her full attention, her eyes soft and filled with compassion. "She said she wasn't sad. That she had a good life and wasn't afraid of dying."

Silvia looked at her brother with slight shock, no doubt because what he had said was out of character for him. He never talked about that kind of stuff. She remained silent, which was out of character for her. She always had something to say about everything, and was quick to say it. Maybe he caught her off guard, or maybe she just wanted to hear what he had to say about the conversation he had overheard.

"It struck a chord with me, I guess 'cause we almost died a couple days ago," Cosmo said, slanting his head and raising his eyebrows. "I mean, before a couple days ago, I never thought of dying, and now I can't stop thinking about it. But not in a morbid kind of way. More as if I'm realizing how weird it is that I've been living my life like it's never going to end. Like it's going to go on forever. It could have ended a couple days ago. Cut short. Yours too."

"But what's it matter how long you have? Isn't quality more important than quantity? I mean, wouldn't you rather have twenty or thirty great years instead of eighty or ninety bad or mediocre ones?"

"I'd rather have ninety good ones."

"What I mean to say is that linear time is just a construct. It doesn't really exist."

"That sounds like something you learned in a college philosophy class," Cosmo said cynically. "Do they even teach philosophy in art school?"

"I have a question for you," she said, disregarding his art school comment. "Are you afraid of dying?"

"I never really thought of it before now. I guess I should be. Isn't everybody scared of dying? Hasn't everybody always been scared of dying? Look at how the Egyptians buried their big shots with all their crap so they'd be all right in the afterlife. I think most of the world's religions formed because of people being scared of dying. I think of all the rich bastards who steal pensions from poor old people are afraid of dying, and having a lot of money is just a way they think they can immortalize themselves. I think it's the reason for war and...."

Silvia cut him off, probably seeing that no real answer coming her way. "You didn't answer my question. And you sound like our little brother going off on some rampage against the government and the world. Who gives a shit if everybody else is scared of dying anyway? The only thing we have any control over is ourselves."

He looked outside the window as if he could find his answer in the nighttime sky. But there was no answer out there, and no answer inside of him. So he gave the only answer he could come up with: "I guess I am. Sure, why not?" He spoke in a most cavalier tone of voice, as if he was making a choice between whether to have French fries or potato salad with his dinner entree.

"Because you don't have to be."

"Why's that?"

"Because not all of you dies. There's a part that goes on."

"That sounds good and all, but how do you know?"

"I don't. It's just what I believe."

"Well, faith doesn't do it for me, Silv. Sorry."

"So you think that all you are is a body? Just a big, stupid body? You think you don't have a soul?"

"I think I don't know. And I don't pretend to know."

She looked up at the ceiling as if frustrated by her brother's unwillingness to see her point, and after only less than a minute she came back with a new angle. "What about that part of you that gets really moved by a song or a painting? That part of you that stays the same, even when your body changes. That's your soul."

"Maybe it is, but I still don't see why having a soul should make me any less scared of dying."

"Because that part goes on when the other part dies. It's indestructible. It can't die." Cosmo still wasn't convinced, and it must have shown in his face. Silvia looked as if she was ready to burst with frustration. "When I paint, that part of me comes alive. I think you don't spend enough time with that part of yourself, and that's why you don't believe in it. If you spent more time living on the inside, you'd start to believe in that thing that we can't see or touch. And then you might not be scared of leaving behind the thing you know as life." And with that, she left to use the bathroom. Cosmo couldn't argue with her last point. If he learned one thing in the past couple of days, it was that he should be spending more time developing his inner life.

When she came back from the bathroom, she continued with the conversation as if it hadn't been interrupted by her departure from the room. "I think most people are afraid of dying because they're living such empty lives, and they're busy trying to fill themselves up with bullshit like nice cars and big houses. If they were really enjoying their time here, they wouldn't feel like they'd been robbed inside, and they wouldn't care about having to leave."

She must have given all it some deep and serious thought. Cosmo recalled his little sister when she was a child. She always had a spaced-out look on her face as if she was somewhere else. Maybe all that time she was thinking about the answers to the big questions about life, the universe, and everything.

"Yeah. That's just like what the lady at the truck stop said." And what the Truck Stop Angel said made perfect sense to him now. He thought about people that were always clinging to the world because they didn't want to let go of it, not because their life here was so great, but because they felt like they should get something more for their time. He thought that a short, fulfilling life must be better than a long, empty one. He considered his own life and how empty it had felt for the past few years. He was young now, so he hadn't thought about death until he almost died. But what if he continued on the same path? Would he end up one of those old people holding onto life like a vine clinging to a fence? Wanting more than what the world could ever give him?

—◆—

The next morning, Cosmo woke to a very bright glimmer of sunlight that seemed to be struggling to get through the tiny crack in the curtains of their room. He got right out of bed with an energy that felt endless, as if he had so much to do and not enough time to do it. He couldn't wait to open the door and look out at the world in the light of day. When he opened the door, he saw a bright sky illuminating the orange and yellow trees in his view. There was a big tree stuffed with songbirds that sang so loudly they woke up Silvia.

"Close the door, Cosmo," she said in a grumpy morning voice. "I'm trying to sleep." As anxious as she was to get to Portland, she wouldn't deprive herself of her precious sleep. So he closed the door and went to the front office where he knew he could get some coffee.

When he got to the lobby, the little old man was putting out some store-bought pastries on a tray. He was dressed in the same sort of outfit and thick glasses that he had worn last night, and he moved around the room taking small, slow steps, his feet barely leaving the floor. Cosmo was in the room for close to a minute before the old man noticed him.

"Good morning," he said to Cosmo. "Help yourself to some coffee and pastries." He scuttled away toward a ringing phone that sat on top of a desk.

Cosmo felt as if he was in some other world in this place that apparently had gotten stuck in time decades ago. He got a cup of coffee and a pastry and sat on a bench outside the office, looking out beyond the parking lot of the motel. Flat earth stretched for as far as he could see. He walked toward the end of the lot to see if there was anything down the road. He turned left and turned right, but both ways he saw the same thing—nothing. He was used to seeing so much in his everyday life. So much stuff crammed into each and every space. The desolate scene before his eyes was clean and simple and pure. The old man came outside of the motel to change the 'Vacancy' sign to 'No Vacancy,' and as Cosmo watched, he felt as if he was watching a video in slow motion. It seemed that every event had its fair share of time to exist here.

Besides the songbirds and the sound of an occasional car, there were no other sounds. He was used to hearing city sounds during all of his waking hours. Sirens, car alarms, voices, and screams all blurring together like one big symphony of noise. But here, every sound was defined and stood alone, and when a small flock of birds suddenly left a nearby tree, the sound of the rustling leaves was amplified in the hollow space.

Cosmo watched the birds fly away and fade into the horizon, and then he went inside to get another cup of coffee and a second pastry. He didn't care that the pastries were slightly stale and that the coffee tasted like it was made yesterday. But Silvia didn't have that same sort of indifference toward the motels breakfast offerings. Cosmo found her in the office by the tray of pastries, looking down at them as if they were rocks the old man got from his driveway.

"They're not that bad," Cosmo said to Silvia as he grabbed one and took a bite from it.

"Yeah," Silvia said, unconvinced. "I'll just eat some of my breakfast bars in the car. I might have some of the coffee though. I wish they had real milk and not this powdered crap to put in it. Maybe I'll go ask him." As she approached the old man, Cosmo felt sorry for him.

"Do you have any milk or cream for the coffee?" She spoke loudly, enunciating every syllable, and pointed at her coffee cup.

"Yeah," he said, pointing to the container of powdered creamer. "Right there. Help yourself."

"No, I mean real milk, like in liquid form," she said.

"No. Just that there." He pointed to the container of powder again.

Silvia said thank you to the man, looked at Cosmo, and said, "I wonder if there's a Starbucks around here."

"Somehow I doubt it," Cosmo said. "That powder crap won't kill you. It's not like you have it all the time."

"It's loaded with trans fats. That's like the worst thing you can put in your body."

"You think too much about all that stuff," Cosmo said. It might have been the first time he had said anything to his sister about her preoccupation with food ingredients.

"Maybe you don't think enough about it," she said quickly back to him.

"You're turning into Mom, you know."

"So what if Mom and I care about what we put in our bodies. I guess we should be like Dad and drink, smoke, and eat crap."

Cosmo didn't bother saying anything back. Instead, he raised his eyebrows, sighed, and looked away from his sister. Clearly, there was nothing he could say that could convince Silvia that she devoted too much time and energy to analyzing every morsel of food she put in her mouth. So he left it alone and switched the subject.

"Do you have the room key? I want to get my stuff together. I'm sure you want to get checked out right away so we can get on the road." He said it in a jaded tone of voice, as though her tendency to rush had become an annoyance that he was learning to accept.

"What's that supposed to mean?" she said, her eyes piercing. She didn't miss a step when it came to her brother.

"What? I just asked if you had the key." He didn't like being dishonest, but sometimes he couldn't help himself.

"Don't pull that passive aggressive bullshit with me, Cosmo Greco. You know I can see right through you." She stood like a warrior, resembling a smaller female version of Frank. She was so amazingly confrontational for being such a little thing.

"What?" he said, half-laughing.

She ignored him and turned away, at which time Cosmo made a look on his face, mocking her and smirking behind her back. It was tough to take Silvia too seriously. She walked toward the room and Cosmo followed her as he assumed that she had the room key.

They gathered their stuff, checked out, and soon were back on the road with Silvia driving and still giving Cosmo the cold shoulder. She turned out of the lot going the wrong way, in the opposite direction of the highway entrance, and although he knew that she went the wrong way, he didn't say anything. He thought her going the wrong way might give him a chance to catch some more of the scenery. And he was right.

They stumbled upon a small area, which had a few boarded up buildings that looked like they might have been businesses at one time. There was a gas station that looked as if it hadn't been in use since the nineteen-fifties, and some old, shack-like houses that looked as if they hadn't been lived in since that same time. The area looked as though it might have been the center of town at one time, and now it was just a dead place. Businesses with no customers. Houses with no residents. In between everywhere else. In between the places that still lived, and some that even thrived and flourished.

"Oh shit," Silvia said who wasn't seeing any of what there was to see. "I think we went the wrong way." She drove up to the next place where she could turn around, which happened to be an abandoned lot with a shack that looked as if half of it had blown away, maybe in some recent dust storm.

Cosmo was glad he'd get another opportunity to see this blown away town gone dead. He wasn't surprised that it took her close to ten minutes to realize they had gone the wrong way. She continued to miss everything around her, and Cosmo thought that even if she hadn't been the current driver, she'd still miss everything around her. He imagined that there was so much racket in her brain about Portland and trans-fats and other nonsense, and that all the racket and clutter kept her missing the world.

Chapter 6

They were greeted in Texas by a 'Don't Mess With Texas' sign and by God himself. God was everywhere—on the radio, at the rest stops, on the billboards by the side of the road. They weren't driving long when Cosmo spotted a giant silver cross that he could see from the interstate. He was happy he was driving so he had the freedom to drive toward it to get a closer look, and that he didn't have to beg Silvia to do so.

"What are you doing?" Silvia asked impatiently as soon as she noticed Cosmo pulling off the highway.

"Don't you want to see that crazy giant cross?" he said, not responding to her implied request to get back on the highway and stop wasting their precious time.

"Oh, that?" she said as if she hadn't even noticed the cross, and even if she did, she couldn't care less about it. "No, not really."

"Well, I do, and it's only, like, minutes out of our way."

And it did, in fact, only take minutes to drive to get to the cross. He pulled over to the side of the road so that he could study it without the distraction of driving. It must have been two hundred feet tall. It stood firm and fierce on the flat, dry ground as if threatening to chase all the non-believers back to Oklahoma. Even Silvia turned speechless as they both stared at the curious object.

"Jesus Christ," Silvia said after a minute or two.

"You can say that again," Cosmo said, staring into the cross as if he expected to see a bloodied Jesus Christ suddenly appear on it.

It appeared to be made of aluminum or some similar material, and the sun reflected off it, making it shine and glow, making it even fiercer than it was on its own. After another few minutes, Cosmo headed back toward the highway. He knew that no matter how long he stared at the cross, he'd never be able to figure it out, so he might as well get back on the road. He was happy to see that the sight was strange and striking enough to get Silvia's attention, and he felt a sense of accomplishment for getting her out of her head for a few moments.

"We're in God country here," she said, staring out the window into the blue sky.

"The heart of the Bible belt."

"Do you think that it became the heart of the Bible belt over time, or it already existed, and then people moved here because of what it was?" Although she didn't express her question very well, Cosmo still knew what it meant.

"A combination of the two."

"I wonder if it has something to do with the heat," Silvia said. "Think about it. All the hot places always seem to corner the market on religion." This was an odd thing to say, but as Cosmo contemplated the existence of the many religions that had their roots in hot places, he thought his sister might have had something.

"The heat can make people crazy," he said. He always thought of religion as a crazy thing. He thought of his own experience with religion and how, even when he was a young boy, he knew that something about it wasn't quite sane. And he thought that the religion he was raised on was one of the more sane ones. He considered the science fiction religions and the frozen-in-time religions. He recalled when he told Frank he was agnostic at age thirteen.

"Well, you'll have to pack your bags and leave then," Frank said seriously when his son informed him of his anti-religious stance. Frank, himself, rarely set foot inside of a church, but insisted that he was, in fact, a good Catholic. Cosmo thought his dad would save religion for when he got old and close to death. He noticed that lots of people went that way.

"I agree that religion can be crazy and lots of people get into it for the wrong reasons, but maybe it helps people. Look at Grandma Tucci. She was a devout Catholic, and maybe she wouldn't have been able to put up with Grandpa if she wasn't," Silvia said. Grandpa Tucci was an angrier and more ferocious version of Frank.

"But maybe she would have left him if she wasn't."

"Possibly, but maybe she would have been scared to leave even if she wasn't a strict Catholic. She didn't really have any marketable skills. I mean, she was a smart lady and all, but she was too busy being pregnant all the time to be anything else but a housewife."

Cosmo thought of Grandma Tucci married to his volatile, hotheaded grandpa. He thought of the plight of the woman at the truck stop, facing her soon-approaching death. He thought of all the tragic things that could happen in a person's life, like when parents lose their children to killers. Maybe religion gave some people what they needed to make their way through this crazy, difficult, and unpredictable world.

"It's not my thing," he said with some sadness in his voice, almost as if he wished that it was something for him.

"It's not my thing either," she said turning in his direction. "But I'm all right with that. I have my own kind of religion."

"What's that?" Cosmo asked. "One that preaches the evils of trans-fats and meat?"

"The night after Grandma died, she came to me," she said, ignoring her brother's attempt at humor. "And in that second, I realized that there was something more than what I could see, feel, and touch. And that's what I have."

And Cosmo knew she did have something. It was that same something that Clay and the Truck Stop Angel had. It was something he didn't feel inside of him for years until this past week. It was something he wanted more of. He knew his newfound want might have something to do with almost dying recently. But the more he thought about dying, the more he knew that he wasn't really afraid of it. He was afraid of going through life without being alive. Fully alive. And that was why he so badly wanted the thing he couldn't name.

He wanted that thing because he saw what it gave to Silvia, Clay, Grandma Tucci, the Truck Stop Angel and all the other people who had it. How they were so alive and how they had a glow about them—a glow that all the sleepwalkers, like himself, lacked. It was something that couldn't be captured or held or contained in any way. It was something beyond sight, sound, or any physical perceptions. It was something beyond scientific proof and most of all, beyond words.

—◂▸—

Around midway through the Texas Panhandle, Cosmo felt the world around him turning west, with dry, dusty winds, vast open space and the occasional tumbleweed. He almost felt as if they should be riding horses instead of in a car. They drove until the sun left the sky and his stomach felt hollow from eating nothing but the pastries from the motel all day. It was time for dinner, and it wasn't long before they saw a sign for a place to eat. The restaurant was a big, brown, boxy place that looked as though it might have been a barn at one time. It looked to be a meat and potato place, which seemed to be the default type of restaurant in Texas. Silvia appeared to be all right with it. She didn't voice any objection as Cosmo pulled into the driveway of the place. She could always get a potato, and if it was covered with cheese, it could almost be a complete meal.

Sure enough, that was just what she ordered—a potato with cheese, sour cream, and chives. It sounded so good that Cosmo got the same thing. He also got a steak and the salad bar option. Silvia suggested that they share the salad bar to save money, but Cosmo reminded her that sort of thing wasn't allowed. He knew she was just trying to get something for nothing. She was always doing that sort of thing, mostly for the sake of getting away with something. She ended up not ordering a salad, but she did fish for some of Cosmo's.

"Looks good," she said inspecting his salad plate.

"Do you want some?" Cosmo asked, knowing what the answer would be. She smiled anxiously and said. "Well, if you insist." Before Cosmo knew it, half his plate of salad was gone. She stopped eating the salad as soon as the server came to bring their food, at which time she started on the potato. Cosmo ate quietly so that he could hear the conversation of the two men at the table next to them. It wasn't difficult because they both spoke loudly, as if they were hard of hearing.

"You been to church today?" One man asked. He spoke in a deep voice and had an accent that was part southern and part something else, which Cosmo could only assume was a western accent with slow-moving, elongated syllables.

"Darlene's been to church," the other man at the booth said in a voice that was barely distinguishable from the first man.

"Well, that's good for her soul," the first man said. "What about your own?" His voice got louder and filled with passion, which got the attention of Silvia, who also began listening to the strange exchange.

"I don't have to worry about my soul. I'm going to heaven."

"Oh, is that right? How's that?"

There was a delay, and Cosmo imagined that the second man had to give the question some thought. Both he and Silvia had their heads leaned over toward their neighboring table, curious. Cosmo was glad for the men being too oblivious to notice them spying on their conversation.

"Because I'm organized," the second man said as if this answer was perfectly reasonable. The first man, however, wasn't buying it.

"Organized?" he said. "They're plenty organized up there."

Cosmo and Silvia looked at each other with smiles and wide eyes as if they couldn't believe their ears. Silvia left the table, saying she had to go to the bathroom, but Cosmo knew she left so she could laugh in private. She was inclined to outbursts of laughter and didn't seem to be able to control them. As soon as she got up from the table, she hunched over and covered her mouth, so that only her laughing eyes showed. The second man could have been Frank in an alternate universe, or Frank if he had been born in the Bible belt. Hearing him talk almost made Cosmo miss Frank a bit, for the goofy character he could be at times. He wondered if his dad was still sad or if he had returned to his old charming, fighting, hell-raising self. He wondered if he was still moping around, or if he had resumed moving about the world as if he was polka dancing; if his eyes were still as despondent as they were the day he and Silvia left for their trip, or if he had gone back to hiding behind a mask of fake celebration.

"I wonder how Dad is doing," he said to Silvia when she returned to the table.

"Did that guy make you think of Dad too?" She leaned in toward her brother.

"Yeah, he did," Cosmo said, gathering a big forkful of salad. "Wonder how he's doing." Cosmo never wondered how he was doing. He never cared. But he had also never seen his dad in such a degenerative state as he had seen him in a few days ago. Now when he thought of Frank, he saw a pathetic, helpless old man, not the angry, crazed monster he was used to seeing. He actually wished that Frank would return to being a monster so that he could stop feeling confused about him. He felt slightly envious of Silvia, who seemed to be free of sympathy for their dad because she had just lived alone with him for several months.

"I bet he's back to his old self," she said as she scooped some food from her brother's salad plate.

"Hey, we should give him a call," Cosmo said, half laughing as if he wasn't totally serious about his suggestion. He almost couldn't believe he made such a suggestion.

"Oh, that reminds me," Silvia said, scrambling through her bag for something. "I have to call Mom. I've only texted her since we left." Cosmo assumed that she thought he wasn't serious about calling Frank. Before he could say anymore, she had her phone out as if ready to dial Donna's number. She then looked down at her phone, smiling, and said, "Emily sent a text. 'Do some stargazing for me in Arizona.'" Silvia looked up from her phone at Cosmo, still smiling, as if she knew that her brother couldn't resist the message from Emily.

"You should stop trying to be a matchmaker, Silv," he said turning serious. "I'm doing all right myself."

"No, you're not," she said, looking him straight in the eye. This was the type of insensitive, blunt remark he'd make, not Silvia. She could be blunt, but not like that. Cosmo wondered if she had made this sort of remark to get back at him for all of the blunt, insensitive remarks he had thrown her way in their lifetime. Although he knew she was right and was probably just trying to help him out in her own way, he felt that he had no choice but to counteract her callous remark with one of his own.

"At least I don't flit from one girl to the next the way you go from one guy to the next," he said smugly.

"Oh, you really got me there," Silvia said, expressionless and bland, as if to say that his remark bounced right off her. Apparently, she didn't care that she stayed with any given boyfriend for short periods before finding a stupid reason to break up with him. At least she had boyfriends. There was truth in the implication of her remark. He hadn't had a girlfriend in years. The only thing he remembered about his last girlfriend was that she was argumentative, and that every time he was with her, he couldn't wait to get away from her. He couldn't even recall her name.

"You know, Cosmo, I'm only trying to help," she said with the slightest bit of compassion in her eyes.

"I know," he said, taking a drink from his Coke. He didn't want to talk about his nonexistent love life with his little sister anymore, so he switched the subject. "Hey, I thought you were going to call Mom."

As soon as Cosmo finished his sentence, Silvia was on the phone to Donna. She didn't waste any time with anything. Cosmo could hear his mom's voice on the other end of the phone: "Hi, sweetheart!" Her voice sounded like a warmer and more cheerful version of the voice that he was used to hearing from her. She also said things that seemed slightly out of character. Things like "I miss you!" and "Are you having fun?" Cosmo had grown to know his mom as nothing but worry, fear, and caution. She never expressed joy at hearing her children's voices or asked about frivolous things like fun. The voice on the phone almost sounded as though it didn't belong to his mom. It sounded as if it belonged to some contented, middle-aged woman who was capable of enjoying her children and her life. This warm, happy voice was now asking to speak to Cosmo.

"Hey, Mom," he said somewhat unsure, as if he was talking to an imposter. But as soon as Donna started talking and asking questions about their trip, he felt more at ease. It felt like talking to an old friend who he hadn't seen in a while. He was glad to hear her voice and to talk to her. She didn't bring him down with cautionary tales and nagging questions as she had done in the past.

"I wish I could be there with you two," she said, longing in her voice. "I've never seen that part of the country. I'd love to see the Grand Canyon. Someday I will." There was also something else that Cosmo wasn't used to hearing in his mom's voice—confidence. Sheer confidence. He wondered if she exuded that same confidence and happiness when he and Silvia were in her apartment. Maybe she had been, and he hadn't perceived the shift within his mom at the time because he was still asleep. He could see it now, even though she wasn't even physically present. It came through loud and clear on the phone. Now he could stop feeling sorry for her. Now the sympathy he had always felt for his mom shifted to his dad.

———

When they got out of the restaurant, the parking lot was full. Apparently, this place was a social hub for people in the area. Cosmo looked up to see a moonless sky crammed full of stars. More stars than he had ever seen through his naked eyes. And he knew there'd be even more once they got away from the light pollution of the town. He kicked himself for not bringing his portable telescope.

As he got to the car, he got a text from his colleague, or ex-colleague, Dario. He couldn't believe that he had only seen Dario just last week, and when he saw his name on his phone, he almost didn't recognize it. He seemed to be from some other lifetime and some faraway place. The text said, 'Looks like you might have been right about our layoff possibly ending. I got word from Liz that we'll be able to get back to work soon!' The lightness in Cosmo's body turned heavy, with most of the heaviness centering right in his gut. He felt like he'd swallowed a bowling ball. The sick feeling in his stomach must have shown in his face.

"What's wrong?" Silvia said from the other side of the car, face squished up like a prune.

"Let's go," Cosmo said as he opened his door. "I'll tell you on the way." After he got in the car, he wondered if he had made a mistake by not telling his sister before they started driving. After seeing the text, he didn't want to keep driving. He wanted the trip to come to a halt so that he wouldn't have to deal with his reality. He didn't want to go back to his mundane life in Philly, and he didn't want to go forward to Portland. Maybe they could settle here in the middle of Texas, work in gas stations and convenience stores, eat cheese-stuffed potatoes, and listen to characters like the Organized Man have nonsensical conversations. Or maybe they could just drive a few miles every day so that they'd reach Portland sometime next year. If only they could become stuck somehow and not have to go on. He thought of Silvia as a girl, wishing their mom would never stop driving all the times they escaped from Frank. Now he understood what she must have been feeling. Maybe her restlessness was somehow contagious. He believed that insanity was contagious, so maybe restlessness was also contagious.

What a weird thought to entertain. He wondered why he was suddenly turning irrational. He had had a lifetime of perfect rationality, and now his brain was turning on him. Maybe he wouldn't be thinking such nonsense if he had a normal response to the text.

A Cosmo response. He was responding as if he was someone else. Had someone taken over his body? This could have been his craziest thought yet —a product of reading too much science fiction. But he wouldn't be grasping for such outlandish explanations if he could understand what was happening inside of him. He lived his whole life knowing just who he was, and now he had changed into another person. Some strange person who was sickened by news that he would have gladly welcomed less than one week ago.

He looked over at his sister who grew impatient at him for not answering her question. He couldn't answer it because he couldn't articulate it. There were no words in his mind, only pictures. He saw his credit card bill, and then he saw his old self sitting at his old desk at his old job. The image looked as though it had a gray, sheer veil draped over it. Beyond seeing this disturbing image, he felt the extreme boredom of his old job. Of course, he didn't know he felt that way when he worked there.

And just as he was feeling the boredom in his bones, he got another flash of the credit card bill. He then saw himself living in Portland, working at some super store like Target or Wal-Mart. Maybe he should get an early plane back to Philadelphia. He could fly back from Los Angeles. Or Phoenix, better yet. He loved Silvia, but he didn't want to become like her. He wanted to remain the person he was, the person he knew.

"Are you going to tell me or what?" Her curiosity seemed to grow. "Your mood changed right after you looked at your phone. You must have got some bummer text or something." She was such a detective.

"I heard from some guy I worked with that the layoff is coming to an end," he said, looking out the window, still not wanting to miss an opportunity to look at the starry sky, even despite Dario's text. More stars cluttered the sky since they left the restaurant parking lot. They were now far away from any artificial light, and the sky was perfectly clear, so there was nothing to cloud his view. He kept looking into the stars, hoping for an answer to the confusion he felt inside himself.

"Isn't that what you wanted?" Silvia asked, sounding even more confused than he felt.

"Yeah," he said, not at all sure of himself, still looking at the stars.

"You don't sound so sure," she said, prompting him for more of a response than an unsure 'yeah.'

He said nothing, hoping in the back of his mind for a shooting star so he could wish away his confusion. He wasn't superstitious, but he now felt as if the possibility of a shooting star was the only thing he had left. He looked over at Silvia, who was waiting for a response, but he didn't know what to tell her. He knew she could never understand his dilemma. She was always ready for the next thing. She never looked back. She only moved forward. Anyway, he didn't want to express any doubt to her, as he thought it might give her a strange sense of satisfaction. As if he was moving over to her side, or something. Soon he might stop eating meat, start painting weird surreal stuff, and buy his own beaten-up car so he could drive from place to place whenever he wanted. He might even become like one of her poor, bohemian, artistic friends. Maybe that wouldn't be so bad. He thought of Clay who fit that description perfectly and who seemed to be living a happy life.

"Well," Silvia said impatiently, prodding him on. He knew she'd never let up, so he gave in, but did so without giving his whole self away.

"Well, maybe I don't want to go back to that job. Maybe I can get something that pays more money." He didn't mention the boredom thing because he knew he'd hear some form of 'I told you so' crap from her. She had never had an opportunity to tell him so, and surely she'd welcome one with open arms. He was always telling her so. That was his job as the sensible, older brother.

"I never once heard you complain about money, Cosmo," she said with suspicion in her voice. She wasn't buying his lie, and for some reason he wasn't prepared for that. He should know better.

"Well, I never talk to you about a lot of stuff." He didn't sound too convincing, but it was the best he could do.

"Mm." She sounded completely unconvinced. He couldn't see the look on her face, but he imagined it was a smug one. He almost couldn't believe that he cared what she thought. He never cared before, and she knew he never cared. Maybe she was sensing his concern for what she thought of him. Now he felt like a girl for the way he was trying to jump into his sister's mind, wondering what she thought and caring about what she thought. He had better turn back before it was too late. Before they got to the other side.

Chapter 7

They stayed in a small motel at the edge of the Texas border. They both wanted to make it to New Mexico but neither could drive any further, and Silvia told Cosmo he should see the New Mexico welcome sign in the daylight. And she was right. It was bright yellow and went perfectly with the brilliant, shining light in the sky. The light here was nothing like he had ever seen before. It was something beyond bright, and it made him feel new and clean inside. Thoughts about the text he got from Dario and about going back early had all been erased, as if the desert sun had burnt them clean from his mind. Going forward felt like the only way to go for now.

Unfamiliar trees lined the sides of the road. Some had branches that were all twisted up inside themselves, shooting off in different directions. Others were stout, plant-like trees with skinny branches reaching up as if to grab onto the sun. Big, black, mystery birds swooped down into the trees and flew away to make huge circles in the sky. Flat-top mountains made of copper-red rock glistened. The morning light passed through every object in his sight, giving them all perfectly defined shadows. Even the highway embankments added to the magical beauty—painted a pale shade of brownish pink with Native American designs carved into them.

Cosmo now understood why Silvia always talked about the surreal type of beauty in this part of the country. He was glad she seemed to be enjoying it, as she looked out the window placidly. He also was glad that she was the current passenger, as this gave her more of a chance to take in their surroundings. It might have been the first time on the trip that she seemed to let go of whatever she was holding onto so tightly. She wasn't talking, fidgeting, or looking worried about something. She was just gazing out the window as if what she saw was all there was.

"I can't wait to get some Mexican food," she said, still gazing out the window.

"I could eat," Cosmo said. They had only coffee for breakfast—stale, bitter coffee that they got at a Circle K convenience store. Quite possibly the worst coffee Cosmo had ever had in his life.

"Well, it's a little early for lunch, but I'll start looking out for places," Silvia said, reaching her arm into the backseat. "In the meantime, do you want a Cliff Bar?" She unwrapped one for herself. They tasted like candy bars to Cosmo, and he didn't want anything sweet, so he asked if she had anything else. She turned completely around so she was facing the backseat and went through her grocery bags.

"Oh, here's something you'll like," she said, taking out a plastic bag filled with something that looked like green chips. She held it up in the air as if it was a prize. The label said it was made of seaweed. Cosmo didn't think he was ready to snack on something made of seaweed. He had tasted seaweed only once in some sushi, and he didn't like it. But this trip was all about trying new things, so he told Silvia that he'd have some. His positive response produced a big smile on his sister's face. She seemed very excited about her brother trying some of her special snack. Her excitement grew when he asked for more. To his surprise, it was tasty, and the saltiness made it strangely addictive. He ate it until he finished the whole bag. He hoped to eat it without getting a lesson from his sister on the many benefits of seaweed, but that was too much to ask for.

"It's loaded with minerals," she said, her body enlivening. "You probably have enough minerals for, like, the whole week now."

"Mm," he said, faking an interest. Of course, she caught him acting. He didn't want to say anymore, because he knew that whatever he said would come out in a mocking way.

"Oh, you seem really convinced," she said facetiously laughing. Her laughter faded as she said, "Look there, Mexican food!" She pointed to a billboard advertising a Mexican restaurant. "Next exit! Oh, yay!" She jumped up and down in her seat like a little kid.

The restaurant was a concrete box, colored off-white and that same pale pink that was everywhere out here.

The inside was dark, small, and only half-full, but that could have been because it was in between breakfast and lunch. A light brown, moon-faced woman greeted them, smiling with big, bright, red lips. She seated them by a small window where Cosmo could look out into the endless sky.

"Now, I know you've never eaten Mexican food before, so I want to tell you about some things on the menu."

She was about to go on when Cosmo cut her off. "I've eaten Mexican food before." He looked up from his menu with a cynical expression and shook his head back and forth.

"Well, Taco Bell doesn't really count," she said, returning his cynicism. She was always reminding him of how worldly she was and how worldly he wasn't.

"I've eaten at places other than Taco Bell, and even if I didn't, I'm sure I can figure it out."

"I'm just trying to be helpful," she said, looking down at her menu, smart enough to desist from explaining the menu to Cosmo. He didn't need any explanations, despite his lack of experience with this type of cuisine. He opened the plastic coated menu and the words "cheese quesadilla" jumped out at him. He wasn't sure what a quesadilla was, but he loved anything that had cheese on it. And just as his mind was set on what to eat, the same lady that greeted them showed up at their table to ask them if they were ready to order.

"You need more time?" she asked in her pleasant, broken-English voice.

"I'll get a chicken and cheese quesadilla and a Coke," he said, closing his menu and handing it to the lady. He looked over at Silvia, who was looking down nervously at her menu.

"Is there lard in the refried beans?" she asked the waitress, still looking down. "Because I can't have any lard. I'm vegetarian." This poor waitress looked less interested in Silvia's dietary requirements than the truck stop waitress had.

"Yes," she said, deadpan face.

"All right, then. I'll just have a burrito with black beans, rice, cheese, and guacamole. No meat."

"Anything to drink?" the waitress asked.

"No, just water," Silvia said, uneasy. "That's no meat in the burrito."

"Yes," the waitress said in an irritated voice. "I heard you the first time."

Cosmo shook his head and rolled his eyes, and as soon as the waitress walked away, he said, "Just hope the cooks don't spit in our food."

"I just wanted to make sure she heard me about the meat thing," Silvia said defensively.

"You shouldn't piss off the wait staff like that."

"Well, I just wanted to make sure she heard me," Silvia repeated, drinking some of her water. "It didn't seem like she did."

Cosmo didn't want to lecture his sister and put a damper on what had so far been a great day, (minus the Circle K coffee.) So instead he took the time to look around at the place. He tried to compare it to something from where he was from, like a diner, but it was different from a diner. It wasn't a regular restaurant either. It had plain, stone walls with a couple of simple paintings of Mexico hanging on them. There were only a few people eating there, and they looked as though they might be the same people who ate there every day.

Within only a few minutes, the waitress brought a round, lidded plastic container. Silvia told Cosmo it was for the tortillas, and of course she got great satisfaction from giving him this bit of information. Following the tortilla container, two big plates full of food with melted cheese were set before them. Cosmo's quesadilla tasted even better than it looked.

"What do you think?" Silvia said taking a bite from her burrito. "Pretty amazing, huh?"

"I love it," he said, putting a big forkful of food in his mouth. "But then again, you could melt cheese on a shoe and it would taste good to me." He didn't quite want to give his sister the satisfaction of knowing that this food far surpassed any Mexican food he had ever had in his East Coast life.

As he looked out the window, he remembered that they were in the Southwest, and knew that he wanted to do something in this part of the country. He couldn't quite remember what it was though. He never forgot anything, so he wondered why he forgot something all of a sudden and could only attribute it to the fact that so much had happened in the past few days that his brain was working overtime processing all the recent happenings. He looked outside the window as if the answer might be out there, and suddenly it came to him.

"Oh yeah," he said to his sister. "That crater is coming up soon."

"Well, it's not that soon," she said pouring some salsa on her burrito. "It's in Arizona. These are big states, you know. They're not like New Jersey." This place sure wasn't anything like New Jersey.

———

As he pulled out of the parking lot driveway, he felt the clutch slip once more. He had to tell Silvia.

"Hey, Silv," he said. "This clutch is going to need to be fixed."

"I'm sure we can make it to Portland."

"I thought you were into taking good care of your car."

"I am," she said. "I just want to wait until we get to Portland."

He knew that trying to convince her was futile, so he dropped the subject. As they drove on, the scenery became even more unearthly, with an increase in ravens, cactus plants, and red rock mountains. Silvia drove while Cosmo looked out at the world. The still-clear sky and flat terrain enabled him to see far, all the way to the mountains, whose shadows had shifted dramatically since the first time he saw them today. He could almost see the shadows moving. He was struck by all of the open space of this place. Even the most built-up place around, Albuquerque, had lots of open space.

They stopped in a town just west of Albuquerque for a bathroom break and to buy a gallon of water. Small white and tan houses made of stone were scattered along the wide-lane roads of the town. When Cosmo got out of the car, he heard nothing but the sound of the desert wind. It was strange and melodious. It sounded close and far away at the same time. It was strong, but it didn't sound like it was fighting with the world around it. It passed through everything in a most unobtrusive way. It made him quiet inside, and through the quiet, he could hear a part of himself that sounded different from his usual dull and cynical inner voice. Although the voice was inside of him, it sounded as if it came from a distance, and he couldn't quite make out what it had to say. Maybe it was just learning how to make words. Or maybe it was beyond words. He always thought that words could say it all, but now he was beginning to see their limitations. So he stopped to listen to this word-less voice.

He listened to the sound of the wind and his inside voice until Silvia came out of the restroom and suggested that they go to the store that was next to the rest stop. He was pleasantly surprised she had suggested something that would delay her arrival in Portland in any way. The shop was turquoise, white, and pink and shaped like a giant teepee. The inside was crammed with everything Native American, or as they said in these parts, 'Indian.' Pottery, jewelry, moccasins, hand-woven baskets, and rugs. They weren't in the store long when a small man with a big yellow mustache popped out from behind the counter and said to Cosmo and Silvia, "You the help?"

"Huh?" They both asked the strange man, puzzled. The man pointed to a 'Help Wanted' sign in the window.

"You the help? I got a call from somebody who said they'd be coming down in response to the ad I put in the newspaper." He looked, talked, moved like Yosemite Sam, and didn't seem like a real person. He was small in stature but big in every other way. His bizarre notion that they had come into his shop in response to a classified ad in a newspaper only added to his animated demeanor. And who still puts 'Help Wanted' ads in the newspaper? Further, it was hard to believe that he needed any help. It seemed as though they were the only two customers who had come in all day.

"We're not the help," Silvia said. Cosmo just stood there, still speechless, still trying to process this strange interaction that was getting stranger by the second. The little man took off his cowboy hat and approached Silvia and Cosmo, saying, "Allow me to introduce myself." Cosmo was expecting him to say 'I'm Yosemite Sam,' and although the man didn't say that, he did give another name that was just as cartoonish. "I'm Crazy Ted."

"I'm Silvia, and this is my brother, Cosmo."

"Hey, nice to meet you," Cosmo finally said. He held out his hand for Crazy Ted to shake. Cosmo couldn't remember the last time he shook a stranger's hand or said 'Nice to meet you' to someone. It wasn't something that was usual in his social circles, which consisted mostly of gamers and geeks who only conversed with each other in a virtual way.

"Suppose you're wondering about my name?" Crazy Ted seemed quite anxious to give them an explanation, almost as if he couldn't hold himself back from talking. "I came out here from Pennsylvania in '79. I was just seventeen at the time. I hitched out. Of course, my parents didn't go for it. But I never belonged back there, and they knew it. I was born a cowboy. When I first got out to the rez, I was known as Crazy White Boy. Later, as people got to know me more, they called me Crazy Ted, with Ted being my first name and all."

When he said that he came from Pennsylvania, Cosmo didn't know what to think. At first, he thought it took away from the romantic cowboy image of Crazy Ted, and then he thought that it just added to his mystique. He tried to imagine him in some suburban Pennsylvania neighborhood, a cowboy that had been misplaced in the wrong family, the wrong place, and the wrong time; a cowboy at heart, wanting to burst out of his skin and be who he was today. He appeared assimilated, speaking with a western accent, calling the reservation 'the rez.' Cosmo calculated his age as being somewhere in his early fifties. That seemed about right.

He didn't have much more time to envision Crazy Ted's past life, as the cowboy continued with his story. "I wasn't out here two months when I met the love of my life. A beautiful Navajo lady with eyes as dark and deep as the blackest night sky." All of a sudden, he turned into a poet. "We had two little girls just as pretty as she was." As soon as Cosmo heard the word "was," he turned sad inside. She was gone, and by the way Crazy Ted turned his head toward the floor reverently, Cosmo assumed that she had died. He was right. "She died two years after our little one, Chenoa, was born. It was a stroke that killed her." He turned his head up and stared right into Cosmo's eyes, and Cosmo could see a glimmer of light in Crazy Ted's face, beneath his right eye. The light grew as he talked on about his dead Navajo wife, whose name was Rosemary. He talked about her as if she had never gone: About the color of her hair, the way she loved the smell of burning sage, how she told their children bedtime stories every night without fail, the way she sung in the shower, and how she made the most delicious fry bread he had ever tasted. He didn't have a trace of sadness in his voice or face. The glimmer of light beneath his right eye overtook his entire face by the time he had finished talking. No sadness there. As he went on about Rosemary, Cosmo could almost see her standing beside her husband, as if his words had resurrected her, or as if she had never left his side.

———

Cosmo couldn't leave Crazy Ted's without buying something, and he wanted to give the storeowner the pleasure of helping him find that something.

"You don't seem like the moccasin-wearing type," Crazy Ted said. He got that right. "Or the jewelry-wearing type, even though I do have some fine men's rings in stock." Cosmo could never see himself wearing a ring under any circumstances, no matter how fine the ring. A tiny piece of pottery caught his eye. It was shaped like a pot with some design etched on it in gray, although he didn't know what the design was or what it represented. But he liked it. It looked like something with wings, but it wasn't a bird. It was some mythological being that could have been living nicely in one of Silvia's paintings if it had been in color. Just as he thought that he'd buy the piece of pottery, Silvia came up to him with a turquoise blue poncho with red and black designs all the way around it.

"Just try it on," she said to him smiling.

"All right," he said as if humoring his sister. He slipped the poncho over his head. He didn't expect to like it, but he did. And even more than liking it, it made him happy.

"Not very Native American," he said quietly to Silvia so that Crazy Ted wouldn't hear him. "More Mexican."

"Well, we are in New Mexico," she said. "One thing's for sure. You won't be going back to Philly in that." Upon hearing his sister say this, he decided to buy the poncho.

"I'll buy this," he told Crazy Ted, who seemed delighted with his choice.

"Which way you headed?" Crazy Ted asked as he rang up the purchase.

"West," Silvia said, like there was no other way.

"You're taking forty through Arizona then?" Crazy Ted asked.

"For sure. Cosmo wants to see a crater, and I want to see the Grand Canyon."

"Well you got to go to Hopi then." Crazy Ted said it as if he had decided this part of their trip for them.

"Where's that?" Cosmo said.

"It's about an hour east of the Canyon. It's another world. Not like any other rez. You're fools to miss it. It's the center of the universe!"

Cosmo and Silvia looked at each other as if it was something they should definitely consider, especially since Crazy Ted called it the center of the universe.

"Sure, we'll check it out," Cosmo said. He had barely finished speaking when Crazy Ted pulled out a map of Hopi. It was the emptiest map Cosmo had ever seen. By the looks of the map, the entire reservation had about five roads, some of which didn't appear to have names. Crazy Ted showed them the way to the three mesas that made up the place and showed them exactly where the center of the universe was.

"They call it Old Orabi," he said, leaning over the map.

"Yeah, well, we'll be sure to check it out," Silvia said, not sounding like she had any intention in to do so. "Thanks for everything." Cosmo could tell that she wanted to get on her way, so he bid farewell to Crazy Ted.

"Yeah, thanks for everything," Cosmo said. He was most thankful for Crazy Ted's story of his undying wife, Rosemary. When they left the store, Crazy Ted followed them out so he could smoke a cigarette. As the two drove off, he waved goodbye to them. Cosmo had a gut feeling that the image of him waving his big red hand in the sky was a picture that would stay with him for the rest of his days.

———

They didn't drive far when Silvia said, "That was some story, huh?"

"Sure was," Cosmo said. "You know something?" He wanted to tell her how he could almost see Rosemary standing beside Crazy Ted, but he felt a little embarrassed. He thought that his being so touched by Crazy Ted's story was a reaction that wasn't within his character, and he was growing tired of questioning his identity. It was too late though. He started something, and his unrelenting sister would surely get it from him.

"What?" she said, demanding an answer. He had to give in now.

"I could almost see her standing there beside him." He said this half-laughing to cover up his seriousness, but Silvia seemed to look right through his cover-up as she disregarded his laughter.

"That's incredible, Cosmo." She said this as if she was congratulating a schoolboy for getting a tough math problem right. He knew her response would be something like that and that his vision wouldn't mystify her or blow her away. How could she be blown away? She kept Grandma Tucci alive in the same way that Crazy Ted kept Rosemary alive.

"It made me think of Grandma," she said with some sadness in her voice. "Lately, I haven't been keeping her with me like I used to. When I grow apart from her, I get further from myself."

"Maybe it was a reminder for you then," Cosmo said. "To think of her more."

"Yeah," she said, not turning away from the windshield. "That's what I think too."

"You're lucky you have that," Cosmo said. When their grandma died, Cosmo felt sorry for his sister's loss. But now he didn't see it as a loss. It was more like Silvia had gained something when their grandma left the earth. Something that would never leave her side.

"I'm hungry," Silvia said, as they were approaching what appeared to be a city.

"Looks like there's stuff ahead," Cosmo said.

"Yeah," Silvia said, looking out the front window as if she wanted to jump out of her seat. "I think it's Gallup." She opened her glove compartment and got out a map. "Yeah, that's what it is. There'll be lots of places to eat there."

They found a place that had a big sombrero on the top of the building, and was filled with people, warm lights, and festive mariachi music—maybe a bit too festive. It was loud, and fast, and didn't match Cosmo's feeling of fatigue from having driven all day. He was glad to find a room in the back that was quieter and less crowded than the rest of the place.

As soon as they sat down at a table, a waiter popped over to take their drink order. Neither of them drank alcohol as a rule. Growing up in a household with a drunk had turned them off to booze. But tonight, the idea of a margarita appealed to Cosmo, so he ordered one. Silvia looked at him as if a second nose had suddenly grown on his face and said, "You're getting a drink?"

"Yeah, just one," he said.

"Well, maybe I'll have one too then," she said looking at the waiter.

"That's two margaritas?" the waiter said.

They both looked up at him and nodded.

"I haven't had a drink in like forever," Silvia said after the waiter had gone. "You know, with Dad and all. I get scared I'll end up like him."

"Well, neither of us has so far, so I don't think we have to worry about it. Besides, I don't think alcoholism is something you can inherit."

"Maybe so," she said, not seeming entirely convinced of her brother's theory. "But I think I heard there is a gene for it. And look at Dad's dad. He was a drunk."

"With Grandma Greco for a wife, it's understandable that he was a drunk," he said, smirking.

"Yeah, well, what about Dad?"

"Maybe there is some genetic component. But I didn't get it and neither did you. And neither did Vince or Angie."

"Sometimes I think Dad was born unhappy," Silvia said, turning serious. "And that's why he drinks."

Cosmo could see his dad's sad face that they had left behind. He always thought of Frank as nothing more than rage and anger, but now he saw him as just sad. Maybe he had concealed his sadness all this time with anger. He used to look big and scary in Cosmo's mind, and now he just looked feeble and lost and sad. Maybe all drunks were just sad beneath their loud and rage-filled selves. This reminded him of something he had heard once about subliminal advertising.

"I heard something once about subliminal ads for alcohol. They'd put skulls in the ice cubes or something."

"So it's like a death wish?" Silvia said, who then continued without giving Cosmo a chance to answer her question. "Well, that makes perfect sense in Dad's case. Once I asked him why he *had* to have a drink, and he said 'Reality's harsh' while slamming one down."

The drinks couldn't have come at a worse moment. They came in two big, wide-rimmed, goblet-shaped glasses, and the waiter placed them down on the table, followed by a basket of chips and a bowl of salsa.

"Are you ready to order?" the waiter asked. Neither of them had even looked at the menu.

"Oh, sorry," Cosmo said to the waiter. He was afraid to tell him that they needed more time because it was a busy place, and he feared that if the waiter went away, he might not come back for a long time. So he opened the menu and looked for something to jump out at him, and that something was chicken fajitas. He didn't know what a fajita was, but it sounded good. He ordered and looked at Silvia, who was nervously looking at the menu. He felt sorry for his sister, as she put so much weight on every decision she made. He always felt annoyed by her indecisiveness, but now he felt sympathy for her not being able to decide about something as insignificant as what to eat for dinner.

"Just pick something and close the menu, Silv. It doesn't have to be the most perfect thing on there." But his advice didn't seem to make much of an impact on her, as she continued staring nervously at her menu. The waiter excused himself and said he'd be right back. Cosmo didn't believe that he'd be right back, but in fact, he was back in only a few minutes. In the meantime, he had finished half of his drink and almost the entire basket of chips.

"I'm sorry," Silvia said. "You're right. I'm just going to pick something." Yet she continued to stare at the menu. Cosmo was sure she had had ample time to read it through several times. He thought he'd give her some help by forcing the menu shut. At this, she looked up at him with frowning lips and saucer eyes.

"You've had time to read everything on that fucking menu. Just pick something already. And don't ask the waiter a million questions." As he said this, the waiter appeared back at the table and looked at Silvia, prompting her for her order.

"I'll just have the chile relleno," Silvia said, looking up at the waiter and handing him the menu. She looked as if she was surprised by her ability to pick something. She also seemed unsure that she had made the right decision. But at least she had picked something and didn't ask the waiter a bunch of questions. Maybe Cosmo did get through to her.

"Good choice," the waiter said, smiling.

"Thanks," Silvia said, as if she was proud of herself for making a choice. She really seemed to need this assurance from the waiter. After he had gone, she took a big sip of her drink and started on the chips and salsa. Cosmo used the time to look at a map on his phone to find the locations of Hopi, the Grand Canyon, and the crater, all of which were in Arizona. The crater was right on the way, but Hopi was a good hour out of their way. He had never heard about the place until today, but he was set on going there, especially after Crazy Ted's review.

"What are you looking at?" Silvia asked as she munched away at the chips.

"A map of Arizona," he said, eyes fixed on his phone. "The crater is on the way, but Hopi and the Canyon might be slightly out of our way." He didn't want to tell her that Hopi was an hour or so out of the way because he knew that she wouldn't go for that. Unfortunately, she asked him for more specifics.

"How far is slightly, Crazy Ted?"

"Like, an hour," Cosmo said. "And why are you calling me Crazy Ted?"

"That's too far, Cosmo," she said, and then continued without any kind of pause. "I called you Crazy Ted because you're talking like him, calling the Grand Canyon, the Canyon. Next thing, you'll be a reservation, a rez."

"Silv, we can't miss the Grand Canyon. Mom would never forgive us. And Hopi is just east of it. Look here." He showed her the map on his phone.

"All right," she said with reluctance. Maybe the drink was helping to loosen her up. She didn't seem as rigid and steadfast as usual.

"Cool," he said, smiling. "We got to go to the center of the universe, little sister."

Not long after, the food arrived. It looked delicious and tasted even better.

—◣◢—

When they got out of the restaurant, Cosmo felt the thin, dry, desert air brushing up against his skin. The sun had gone, and its departure turned the sky brilliant shades of pink and orange. He looked just past the small dirt parking lot of the restaurant to see the silhouette of a fat, sombrero-wearing man stumbling by them and fading into the sky, the color of which changed from brilliant pink to deep blue right before his eyes. Maybe it was the thin air or maybe it was the tequila, but as he watched the fat man fading into the horizon, he thought this had to be the most beautiful place on the planet.

Chapter 8

They spent the night in some cheap motel in Holbrook, Arizona. When Cosmo got out of bed, he opened the drapes to see an overcast sky filled with big, billowy, white puffs that drooped down, touching the horizon in spots. He went outside to see that the overcast sky wasn't dreary or gray, but that a bright light filled every space around him. The overcast sky even lent to the beauty of the desert, as he could see everything more clearly. No glare or reflections. Just pure pictures. Silvia was still sleeping, so he could have some time to wander around alone, perhaps go to a nearby rock shop that he had spotted last night.

He put on his poncho, reached for his baseball cap out of habit, and put it on his head. He felt it squeezing his head, and as he looked at himself in the mirror, he noticed how his hair popped out of the hat. His thick, curly hair trapped and contained with the rest of him. He had worn a hat every day for the past few years in order to contain his hair, so that he would not stand out. But he no longer had any need to hide, so he took it off and threw it out.

He headed across the street to the rock shop. The shop sat between a taqueria and a small no-name grocery store. Too bad it was closed. It was only nine in the morning though, so it made sense. He saw the sign on the door that said it would open at ten. Silvia could sleep at least that long. Cosmo looked inside the little shop through one its windows to see shelves and tables crammed with boxes of all kinds of rocks and crystals. He saw some handmade signs posted in various places and noticed one that said meteorite rocks. He was reminded of the fact that soon he'd be seeing the crater and felt a wave of excitement go through him.

He went into the taqueria and ordered huevos rancheros. Only a week ago, he wouldn't have known about the existence of huevos rancheros or anything like it. When he first arrived out west, he felt like an outsider or an observer. But now he felt like a part of his surroundings. As he sat waiting for his breakfast, looking out a small window onto the open desert space, he thought about what he'd be doing only less than one month ago at this time. He'd be walking down a crowded, cluttered, city street on his way to his job. After he arrived there, he'd be sitting behind his dull and bland desk. In fact, his whole life in Philadelphia was dull and bland, and in his mind's eye, it looked like a black and white movie. How could he go back to black and white now that he had been living in color? Sure, it had only been less than one week since he had been on the road, but it felt like a lifetime. When he thought of returning to that same old, colorless existence, he felt almost sick inside. Like he'd rather go work at the rock shop next door than go back to his office job. Or better yet, work with Crazy Ted. The 'Help Wanted' sign at Crazy Ted's flashed in his mind. He smiled and laughed inside when he imagined himself going back to work for the little cowboy.

"Why didn't you wake me up?" Silvia said as soon as Cosmo came back to the room. She rushed around, gathering her things, and looking around the room as if to check to be sure she had all her belongings.

"I know how much you love to sleep," Cosmo said as he gathered his own belongings with less than half the amount of speed and ambition as his sister.

"Well, we have a lot to do today if you want to see the crater, Hopi, and the Grand Canyon." She continued with a pleading face, "Unless we can cut something out."

"Oh c'mon, Silv," he said, collapsing on a chair in the room. "I am doing you a favor by coming on this trip. The least I can get out of it is seeing a few sights in a state that I'm sure I'll never visit again."

"All right already," she said as she continued to gather her things. "Let's get a move on then."

Cosmo was all ready to go, so he got the room key and said he'd check them out and meet her back by the car. As he walked to the motel office, he noticed something different about how his body felt. Lighter. The bounce that had gone away from his step for years had now returned. And without the constraint of a hat, he bopped his head back and forth freely as he used to do.

"You walk just like your Uncle Vincent," Donna used to say to him all the time. Because he loved his Uncle Vincent, he kept up the bouncing and bopping. But these motions drifted out of his body just in the past few years. He was glad that this part of him had now returned.

━━

Cosmo wasn't surprised that Silvia had several questions about the crater. She was lazy when it came to doing things like reading the plaque near the crater that would have easily answered all of her questions.

"How did it get there?"

"A meteor fell to Earth."

"When did it fall to Earth?"

"About 49,000 years ago."

"How wide is it across?"

"Almost a mile."

"How deep is it?"

"Almost 600 feet."

"Why is it so big?"

He was almost reluctant to answer the last question as it didn't seem worthy of an explanation and it should have been obvious to her. So he just looked at her as if to tell her she was too smart for such a stupid question.

"Hey, I'm no scientist." That was certainly true. So he answered the question in layman's terms.

"Some meteors are really, really big, like the one that hit here. And meteors travel through space really, really fast, so when they hit something, they make a really, really big impact, especially if they're gigantic, like this one was," he said, without being condescending. He wasn't one for condescension. She appeared satisfied with his simple answer. He was glad he had a few moments to study the crater, to look at it, and imagine the meteor that made it—to imagine its incredible size and speed. He looked over at Silvia who seemed more than ready to go, so he gave the giant hole one more look, and they were off.

The ride up to Hopi wasn't the smooth, easy interstate highways to which they had grown accustomed. It was a skinny, two-lane highway, and it passed through a Navajo reservation that surrounded the Hopi reservation like a moat surrounding a castle. The Navajo reservation was just what Cosmo had imagined a reservation to be. Sad, stark, and poor. So poor. The earth looked dry and infertile. The few people he saw looked broken and weathered. He saw one person passed out in front of a storefront, and imagined that there'd be plenty more passed out drunks had it been night or even later in the day.

"So sad, huh?" Silvia said as she glanced out the window.

"Yeah, terrible," Cosmo said, sympathetic voice. "They really got screwed over."

It was a depressing place, despite the fact that it was just as light and bright as the spaces that surrounded it. The sadness came through loud and clear. But almost as soon as they entered Hopi, the sadness of the Navajo reservation seemed to lift a bit. Cosmo attributed this to his excitement about seeing the place. It was tough not to be excited after Crazy Ted's rave review of the place.

They were lost as soon as they got there, but Cosmo was eventually able to navigate with the very simple

182 • Grace Mattioli

map. They drove up a road that curved along glimmering white rock mountains. On the other side of the road, there were hills of dried up brown grass with plain, shack-like houses and handmade signs for jewelry, kachina dolls and pottery scattered about.

"Let's go check out one of the shops," Silvia said. She seemed to have relaxed since they entered Hopi, and this was apparent by her suggestion to check out one of the shops.

They followed a sign to a house that contained a store—a small room with shelves lined with dolls, pottery, and glass cases filled with jewelry.

"Welcome," the apparent storeowner said. He was a stout, middle-aged man with black, squinting eyes, high cheekbones and a thick head of hair.

"Hi," Silvia and Cosmo said at the same time, both smiling.

"First time to Hopi?" the man said, smiling back at them.

"How did you guess?" Silvia said, half laughing.

"Just a hunch." A woman came out as he spoke. Cosmo guessed that they were married, and he was right.

"I'm Leonard, and this is my wife, Rachel," the man said, gesturing to the woman.

"I'm Silvia, and this is my brother, Cosmo," Silvia said.

"I can tell you're brother and sister," Rachel said.

"I'm not sure whether to take that as a compliment or not," Cosmo said in a joking way. Silvia rolled her eyes.

"That's our inlay jewelry," Leonard said to Silvia, who was looking inside one of the glass cases. "Can I show you anything?"

"Oh no, I'm just looking," she said. Cosmo was sure she'd have asked him to take out whatever it was she was looking at if she had money to spend. Unfortunately for Silvia, she never had money to spend on anything frivolous because all her money went into her relocation expenses.

"Why don't you look at something, Silv," Cosmo said.

"I better not," she said, then something inside of her seemed to change, and she looked up at Leonard and said, "Well, all right. Can I see that one?"

Leonard took out one of the silver chains with a small pendant and handed it to Silvia. Her eyes lit up when he gave her the necklace, and before she even tried it on, Cosmo decided to buy it for her. When she put it on and stared at herself in the mirror with longing eyes, he knew that he had made the right decision. He only hoped that it wasn't too expensive.

"How much is it?" Cosmo asked Leonard.

"Only thirty-nine dollars," Leonard said.

"We'll take it," Cosmo said.

"Cosmo!" Silvia said, as if to tell him that he shouldn't spend the money on her. But he had already taken out his credit card and given it to Leonard.

"Thank you so much, Cosmo," she said, looking at him with a big smile and gracious eyes.

After they made the purchase, Rachel showed them the studio in which they made the necklace. The studio was a small room connected to the storefront. A hand-made, wooden, worktable with a machine that had a needle on its tip stood in the center of the room.

"This is how we carve the designs in our inlay jewelry," she said, pointing to the needle on the machine. "We Hopis are famous for our inlay jewelry and of course for our kachina dolls." She led them back to the tiny storefront to show them the dolls standing on the shelf. They weren't typical dolls that were meant to be played with by children. They were stout human figures made of wood, wearing Native American costumes and big painted masks.

"Kachinas are spirits of our tribes," Rachel said.

"Cool," Cosmo said, studying one that wore wings made from feathers on its arms.

"This one is called the Eagle Kachina," Rachel said, getting the doll down and handing it to Cosmo. As he studied the detail in the doll, he imagined an artisan carving it and sewing its clothes. He could only imagine how gratified the artisan must have been with the finished product.

"You on your way to the cultural center?" Leonard asked.

Cosmo and Silvia looked at each other as if they weren't sure where they were headed. They had no definitive direction planned.

"Should we be?" Silvia asked.

"Yeah," Leonard said. "You can see the museum, get some lunch, and get tickets for the walking tour." It sounded like he had their whole itinerary planned out.

"Sounds good," Cosmo said.

Leonard gave him directions, and they were on their way. The cultural center was in a pale pink stone building with a museum, gift store, and restaurant inside. The museum was a dark room filled with relics of Hopi culture. They passed through it quickly and were on to the gift store, where Silvia got tickets for the walking tour. Cosmo went straight to the book section. He grabbed a book of Hopi proverbs and turned to a random place in the middle of the short book to see what would pop out at him. He found a proverb that said, 'In death, I am born.'

"C'mon, Cosmo," Silvia said, who had purchased the tickets for the walking tour. "We have to go now if we're going to catch this tour."

The tour group consisted of the tour guide, Silvia, Cosmo, and a couple from Australia. The tour was up a dirt road with small brown and beige houses and some half-fallen metal fences. Natives were scattered about the village in front of houses, many selling their crafts. As the small tour group walked up the road, it terraced into a narrow rock table lined with small white stone houses, unchanged for centuries. Automobiles weren't allowed on this part of the mesa. There was no electricity or running water in the houses. They used fire for light and warmth, and a nearby well for water. Cosmo looked inside one of the houses and saw nothing but a table and very basic, very old gas stove. An older woman came out of the house in a black dress, and she reminded Cosmo of the old Italian women he had seen occasionally in South Philly. She had sheets of white construction paper in her hand and ran toward the tour group with urgency.

"These are from my grandson," she said, showing them some very simple sketches made by a child. "Do you want to buy one? They're only a dollar." The woman showed them five different sketches.

"I'll take these three." Silvia selected three of the drawings and gave the lady three dollars.

As she looked down at the child drawings, Cosmo remembered Silvia's latest ambition to become an art teacher. She went through career ideas like she went through places, but Cosmo hoped that she'd settle on this art teacher idea. He knew that she'd be a great at it, and he could imagine school children adoring her.

Old Orabi, the so-called center of the universe, was the last mesa they visited. Like the other two mesas, it rose abruptly out of the flat, desert land, and on the top there was a group of brown stone houses formed in a circle.

"This part has been continuously inhabited since 1050 AD," Silvia said, as if she was proud of having known that fact.

"How did you know that?" asked Cosmo.

"I heard some lady in the gift store say it."

They saw some children playing outside of one of the houses, and Silvia smiled at them. The children smiled back at Silvia and came up to her as if curious and excited to see someone from somewhere else. They smiled with ease, as if being poor didn't bother them in the slightest. Cosmo thought that they were lucky in a way to be ignorant of all the material things that well-off children in his world quest after. They didn't need the latest high tech gadgets to be happy. They were happy just to play in the sun.

"Hi," one of the little girls said as she looked up at Silvia. "Where are you from?" She had black, almond-shaped eyes that glistened in the light of the sky. Cosmo was surprised by the little girl's openness.

"I'm from far away," Silvia said. "The far east side of the country." Silvia was always kind of ashamed to say that she was from New Jersey, but surely that wasn't the case here. Maybe she thought that the little girl had never heard of this place.

"A state called New Jersey," Cosmo said to the little girl, as if it was some exotic place.

"Oh, I know New Jersey," the little girl said, standing tall and proud. "We learned about it in school."

A woman who looked to be in her early thirties stuck her head out of a door of one of the houses.

"Mae," called the lady from the house. At this, the little girl turned around and yelled back to the woman. "Coming, Mama!" She turned and looked back at Silvia and Cosmo and said, "Want to come see our kachina dolls?"

"Sure," Cosmo said.

Mae led Cosmo and Silvia to the front doorstep of her house where her mom stood.

"Hi there. I'm Linda," the woman said through a forced smile. She had the same black, almond-shaped eyes as her daughter, but they were not young and curious like Mae's eyes. They were tired eyes that had the look of hardship and struggle in them. "Come in and see our dolls." It seemed that everyone here made something.

Silvia and Cosmo greeted Linda and entered a room that was dingy, messy, and filled with worn furniture. An old woman sat on a couch off to the side of the room. It must have been the grandmother. Both Cosmo and Silvia greeted the wrinkled little woman and she returned their hello with a warm smile and cheerfully squinting eyes. In the center of the room stood a little rustic wooden stand with some kachina dolls on top of it. Cosmo wished that he could buy them all, but at this point, he couldn't afford to buy one, unless of course he was going back to his old job. The idea still depressed him.

"They're beautiful," Silvia said as she admired the dolls. She appeared to be studying one of them, maybe trying to figure out the technique used to make them. Mae stood next to Silvia, looking at her admirably. The little girl had taken a shine to her.

"They sure are," Cosmo said, still feeling bad for not being able to buy one. The family wasn't being forceful about making a purchase, and this made Cosmo feel even worse.

"I really wish we could afford to buy one," Cosmo said to Linda.

"Oh, don't worry about it," Linda said. "Just happy you could take a look."

As Cosmo and Silvia walked out, Mae followed as if she didn't want them to leave. Silvia took her phone out of her bag, handed it to Cosmo, and said, "Take a picture of Mae and me." Silvia put her arm around the little girl and they both smiled big for the camera.

As he snapped the picture, he felt some sadness inside. He would miss Hopi. It was like no place he had ever been. A place where people live on dust and empty spaces, on stories and tradition, on their crafts, and on the light and love that filled the air. With all of its poverty and desolation, it didn't feel like a sad place. Perhaps because its people were so tied to that world beyond sight.

They arrived at the entrance of Grand Canyon National Park around four in the afternoon, and were slightly upset about not having more daylight left. Still, neither would have missed or shortened their time at Hopi.

"We'll just make the most of the time we have," Cosmo said to Silvia optimistically.

"Yeah," Silvia agreed, looking out the window with eagerness.

"We'll catch the best part anyway," he said. "Sunset."

They drove right to the south rim as the park ranger who greeted them had instructed. The magnificent Canyon opened itself up to the sky, which was half deep blue and half filled with clouds. The clouds hung around the mountains as if they were formed to each other. Light came through the cloudless spaces in thick, bright strips and turned the Canyon iridescent shades of pink, red, brown and orange. Each time the light shifted, the picture changed dramatically. Cosmo thought it wouldn't amaze him, but he was wrong.

As he stood and stared out at the wonder, a bald eagle flew by him, only a few feet in front of where he stood. He couldn't believe that the creature had flown so close to him. It landed on a ledge for a few seconds and then took off again, its wingspan reaching across nearly the whole of Cosmo's field of vision. Silvia stood right beside him, watching the eagle as it flew over their heads. Neither spoke a word until it flew away and disappeared behind a cloud.

"Wow!" Silvia said. "An eagle. I love eagles!" She looked like she wanted to start jumping up and down.

"Yeah," Cosmo said, still staring at the final trace of the majestic bird. "I don't think I've ever seen one so close."

"Don't you want to know why I love them so much?" she said, disregarding her brother's comment.

"Why?" Cosmo asked as if humoring his sister. "Because you're such a patriot?" He laughed, knowing well that it wasn't the correct answer.

She looked back at him snidely and said, "Because of what they mean."

He didn't say anything. He knew he didn't have to. He knew his sister would tell him the answer without being prompted to do so.

"Strength, courage, immortality, spirit, divinity," she said, gazing into the spectacular gorge below.

He knew about eagles symbolizing courage and strength, but not about immortality, spirit and divinity. The picture of the eagle was still fresh in his mind, gracefully sweeping over the earth, its wings spread like an angel. Divinity seemed to fit just right as something that this phantom bird should symbolize. It shows itself to the world for very short periods of time, here and there. It glides along with unearthly grace to remind everyone that our own journey can be as smooth or as rocky as we chose to make it. It appears and then it disappears as if by some divine magician, and in its brief appearance, it gives the world a flash of revelation. It transcends this world as a reminder that everyone has the potential to rise above.

He thought of Clay writing his songs and of Silvia painting. He saw the strength in the dying woman's eyes in the truck stop and the love in Crazy Ted's eyes for his wife. He saw the near death accident that he and Silvia had less than a week ago. The truck that almost killed him; the truck that opened his eyes. He knew that his openness to all of their experiences in the past few days wouldn't have been without this fortunate incident. He knew that without that occurrence, he wouldn't have discovered the eagle that lived within him.

He looked into the sky that had bluish pink light coming through the clouds, and felt grateful for the beauty before his eyes. Then he felt grateful for having the sight to see it, and for having a tenacious little sister who dragged him out here. He looked over at her to see her staring back at him, almost as if she didn't recognize him.

"You've changed, Cosmo," she said, looking up at him, admiration in her eyes.

The ride down to Flagstaff was in the dark, but even with the dark sky, Cosmo could see the shadows of the giant mountains around him. They were both starving during the entire drive down, but Silvia was determined not to stop for food until they reached Flagstaff, which she claimed had all kinds of great places to eat. The first thing they saw, after entering the town, was an Italian restaurant. The thought of Italian food in Arizona didn't sit well with Cosmo, but he was so hungry that he insisted they check it out.

"I don't know why we're stopping here. There are so many good places to eat downtown," Silvia said as they pulled into the parking lot of the restaurant. They got out of the car and looked in the front window to see that the place was empty inside. Not one person.

"That's a bad sign," Silvia said as she glared through the window into the empty place. "Mom always says that if a restaurant is empty, stay away."

Cosmo knew that she was right, but he felt strangely curious about the place, so he continued staring into the window. As he was about to say that they should leave, he saw a man who appeared to be affiliated with the restaurant in some way—the owner, the cook, or the manager. Maybe a combination of all three. The man saw them staring through the window and he started approaching them as if to encourage their patronage. Silvia must have also seen the man see them as she said, "Oh shit. There's somebody. Let's get out of here!" She was half-laughing as they both ran back to the car.

"Why don't ah you wanna eat ah my food?" Cosmo said in a fake Italian accent, mocking the poor man. Once they were in the car, Silvia let out one of her big, mighty laughs that filled every inch of space inside of the car. Cosmo started the car and they drove away before the man had a chance to come outside in the parking lot. They drove into the downtown that was a few short blocks long and consisted of a mixture of old western and Victorian architecture. Cosmo could easily imagine cowboys roaming the streets, riding their horses through the town, entering saloons through swinging doors, having shootouts at sunset, and frequenting brothels filled with ladies dressed in frilly, lacy, low-cut dresses.

This once wild western town had transformed into a quaint town with cafés, eateries, and souvenir shops that carried a variety of Native American crafts and Route 66 memorabilia. Silvia knew just where to go when they got there. It was a place in what appeared to be the center of the town, on San Francisco Street, and she claimed that they had the best veggie burgers that she had ever had.

"Veggie burgers. Now that's exciting." Cosmo said, mocking his sister.

"They have really good turkey burgers too," she said.

"Oh, boy. Now I don't know if I can contain myself." Silvia sneered back at her brother as if to say that she didn't find any humor in his sarcasm.

The inside of the place was filled with small, wooden tables, warm, dim lighting and hippies, artists, and intellectuals. These were Silvia's people, and she seemed right at home from the second they stepped inside the place. They sat at a table in the center of the room and spent the time before the food arrived, people watching and eavesdropping. Cosmo gathered, from the looks of the crowd and from the fragments of conversation, that there was a university in this town and that it was a place where people came to ski. He also figured that it was somewhat of a tourist destination with its proximity to the Grand Canyon. He liked it here and hoped that his sister knew of a place to stay in this town.

"So, do you know any places we can stay tonight?" Cosmo said after their food arrived.

"There's a youth hostel only a couple of blocks from here," she said, sipping some water.

"A youth hostel. Do we have to do chores?" Cosmo smiled a goofy smile and made his eyes big.

"It's not like that," she said, taking a bite from her beloved veggie burger. "People don't have to do chores. I stayed in youth hostels all through Europe." Any excuse to remind him of her worldliness—a quality which she had acquired only about two or three years ago when she backpacked through Europe and started moving all over the country. Before that, she was as provincial as he was.

———

The hostel reminded Cosmo a bit of his college dorm, and even made him nostalgic for his college days. He dropped right before his junior year. For the first time since he was in college, he felt a twinge of regret for dropping out. Frank had helped him with tuition for two years and then told him that he'd have to do it on his own. He was grateful that his dad had helped him at all, but knew that Frank's help wasn't purely altruistic. He suspected that his father's main motivation in helping his son was so that he could brag to his friends and colleagues that he had a son in an Ivy League school. When Cosmo dropped, Frank told him, "I knew you'd never add up to anything." He seemed to get more joy from being able to resume his role of degrading his son than bragging to his friends about his son attending a prestigious school.

When Frank told him he'd have to pay his own way, Cosmo imagined himself going on financial aid and having to pay off huge loans once out of school. Maybe he'd get a well-paying job or maybe he wouldn't. For some reason, he imagined the latter scenario was the more likely one, which meant that there was a good chance he'd end up broke. He couldn't move in with Frank as Silvia had done. Frank probably wouldn't allow him to move in, and if he did, they wouldn't last a day together under the same roof. The whole thing just felt too uncertain, too unsafe. Shortly after Frank told Cosmo to apply for financial aid, a friend of his told him about a job. So he applied and he got it and he stayed for over eight years.

Now as he sat in this room amongst a bunch of back-packers, he recalled what it felt like to be in school, to learn new stuff every day, every hour, every second, to feel his mind expand like the very universe that he studied in his courses. Shit! Why did he ever drop? What began as a twinge of regret grew into something huge and overtook him. He was too old and too set in his ways to go back. He felt that he had made the biggest mistake in the world. He fantasized about going back in time and doing things differently, and this made him feel even worse. Being alive hurt. That might have been part of his reason for staying dead for so long. And as he sat, kicking himself, calling himself a fucking idiot for dropping out, Silvia appeared at the door of his room to ask if he wanted to get some coffee.

"Not just any coffee," she said. "This is, like, the best coffee in the world."

———

Silvia might have been right too. Cosmo couldn't recall tasting better coffee in his life. They sat toward the front of the café right next to an antique, chrome, coffee roaster, drinking coffee with cream and brown sugar. Silvia got decaf because she was afraid that she wouldn't be able to sleep if she had regular. "We have a big day tomorrow," she warned as Cosmo went for his second cup. "You'd better get decaf too." He agreed, but when he got to the counter, he ignored his sister's advice and got regular coffee.

"Do you ever have regrets?" he asked her as soon as he sat back down at the table.

"No," she said. Probably because she was too busy thinking of the future to go into the past. People who spent time regretting were stuck in the past. "Mom regrets a lot. Maybe you take after her. One time I heard her beating herself up for putting Vince in kindergarten too early. He was already in fourth grade at the time, and he was doing great in school, but she thought for some reason that he was showing signs of being in a class that was too advanced for him. And she just couldn't let it go. I heard her talking to Dad about it one night, and he says to her 'You shouldn't feel so bad. You didn't kill anybody.' I thought that was one of the craziest things I ever heard Dad say. But I think it helped her, because I never heard her talk about it anymore after that. So maybe you should start thinking that way too. Like, maybe you fucked up, but you didn't killed anybody." She laughed and Cosmo laughed too, and with his laughter he was able to forget his regret of dropping out. Frank's crazy wisdom came through for him. After all, he never did kill anybody.

"So what about Hopi," Silvia said, changing the subject. "It's really another world, huh?"

"Yeah, it sure is," Cosmo said, sipping his coffee. "Maybe I'm romanticizing the place a tad, but it seemed like the people there were happy in a way. It's such a poor and desolate place, but it didn't feel sad to me."

"It didn't feel sad to me either. I'm sure it has something to do with the fact that they have their art."

"Why does art make people happy?"

Silvia looked stumped, but within a few seconds, she came up with something. Sometimes she just talked, and as she talked, an answer would form. "It's not that art makes people happy necessarily. It's that people who create have an outlet, a way to break free and transcend this crazy world. It's like what I was talking about the other night. When I paint, I get in touch with that higher part of myself. I think it's the world that takes me away from this part of me."

"You mean your soul?" Cosmo said. Silvia looked back at her brother as if she didn't know who he was. He couldn't blame her. He was sure that she had never heard him say the word soul. He couldn't remember the last time he had said the word either. It was probably sometime in high school or elementary school, and he had said it as an answer to some question in religion class.

"Yeah, my soul," she finally answered his question.

Cosmo couldn't sleep well, and as he tossed and turned, he could hear Silvia warning him to get decaf instead of regular. As he lay awake in bed, he thought about the whole soul thing. Was it something that had a memory? Would his soul be able to remember looking at the stars, learning to play the violin, eating ravioli dinners with his family, and the first time he kissed a girl? Was it something that had opinions? Did it like the same stuff that he liked if it was a part of him? If it had no memory, how could it have any connection to him as a person, and if it didn't have any connection to him as a person, why should he care about it in some afterlife? Now beyond wishing he had stayed in college, he also wished that he had studied philosophy.

He fell asleep tossing these thoughts about his soul around and assumed he might have some kind of illuminating dream that would answer all of his questions. But he had none; at least, none that he could remember. So he woke feeling just as confused as when he went to sleep. But his quest to figure it all out had faded for the moment, as now all that he could think of was getting some of the delicious coffee from the café that they went to last night. He knew Silvia would still be sleeping, and he knew that she'd want a cup of coffee when she woke up, so he bought her one to go. Shortly after he got back, they were on the road. Silvia had decided that they'd make it all the way to Vince's in Berkeley by tonight.

"How far is Berkeley from here?" Cosmo said.

"Only like twelve hours," she said as she drank some of her coffee.

"Only twelve hours," Cosmo said in a mocking voice. "That's really far. We might not make it."

"Oh no. We'll make it." She had determination in her voice, and he knew that saying anything contrary to her plan was pointless, so he stayed quiet and drove onward.

Chapter 9

Winds became stronger with each mile as they entered the California high desert. The red, pink, and white colors, so prominent in the previous two states, faded to several shades of brown and dull green. Windmills, big like giants, sprouted up on hills of dried up grass. Nothing but dust, wind, and wide-open space. But Cosmo thought it interesting and even beautiful in a strange way. He wondered what his little sister, the painter, was seeing in all this. He glanced over at her sitting in the passenger seat. She looked like she was somewhere else. Probably dreaming of her new life in Portland.

He wondered why, with all of her wisdom and philosophical ramblings about the soul, she couldn't seem to live her life. She chased rainbows, started over, looked to the next day, missed the only day she had, never heard the birds sing, and never smelled the roses. Maybe having it all figured out was overrated. He might have felt lost and confused, but at least he could see what was in front of him.

"This is something, huh?" he said.

"What's something?" she said as if she had no idea what he was talking about.

"This high desert place with its crazy strong winds and big, scary windmills."

"Yeah." She didn't sound at all interested in his talk of the high desert.

"You sound impressed."

"Well, what do you want me to say, Cosmo? I've seen all this before. I don't think much of this whole Mojave Desert. I got a flat tire out here once when I was driving alone. It was fucking terrifying."

"How come we didn't take the way through L.A. then?"

She turned to look at him as if he was suggesting that they drive to the moon.

"It's longer, for one thing. And it's nothing but cars and traffic and plastic sunshine for another."

"I guess that answers that question." He ignored Silvia's jaded perception of the area and enjoyed it on his own. It wasn't as scenic as the last two days of the journey, but it was striking in its own way, and it was definitely not like any place he had ever been. The day was clear and blue, so the night would be great for star-gazing. Too bad Silvia was intent on making it all the way to Berkeley tonight where the light pollution would ruin his view of the stars.

"You really want to make it all the way to Berkeley tonight?" he said, making a tired face.

"Yeah, Cos," she begged. "At the very least, we could stay in Santa Cruz. I have a friend there. We can crash at her place."

"What do you have friends all over this country?" he said, partially laughing.

"Well, what can I say."

He was getting ready to ask her about staying in Santa Cruz when he felt something weird in the clutch pedal. It slipped, and when he tried to shift into gear, nothing happened. He remained in the same gear, and the car made an abrasive, grinding noise.

"I told you your clutch was worn," he said as he looked out on the highway, hoping for a rest stop sign.

"I never noticed anything," she said defensively.

He felt like saying that she never noticed anything because she was too busy running around, planning her next move, and staying lost inside her head. But he said nothing. Instead, he continued to look out on the highway for a sign. He could see one a mile or so ahead. As he got closer to the sign, he saw a picture on it indicating that there was a gas station at the next stop.

"I'm getting off at the next stop," he said. Silvia said nothing. He could feel her nervousness permeating the air.

"We're lucky to find a gas station out here."

"I know. I know," she said. But she didn't seem to care about their luck in finding a gas station. It was about a mile off the exit, and when they got there, Silvia insisted on driving the car around the parking lot of the gas station, as if she'd fix it by driving it around. Maybe she wanted to check it herself to see if Cosmo was wrong.

"That sucks," she said, getting out of the car. "I don't know how I never noticed anything was wrong before."

Cosmo didn't say anything but knew that if she bothered keeping one foot on the ground, she might have noticed how bad it was before. If she hadn't been in such a mad rush to get to Portland, she might have paid more attention to his observation about her worn clutch earlier in the trip.

"You have to get it fixed right away," Cosmo said. "We can't go the rest of the trip with it like this." She agreed reluctantly, so they asked the gas station attendant where the nearest repair shop was located.

"Wow," he said through his crooked, yellowed teeth. "There's not much around here. You'd be best to get to Bakersfield and find something there."

"How far is Bakersfield?" Silvia said, sounding desperate.

"Only about forty-five minutes," the man said as he looked at the clock on the wall. "It's not even four now."

"Thanks a lot," Cosmo said.

The drive to Bakersfield was mostly silent but not so peaceful, for Cosmo could feel Silvia's angst growing by the second. After about twenty minutes of driving, she blurted out, "I don't know how I'm going to afford getting my car fixed now."

"I thought you said that you had, like, three thousand dollars saved," Cosmo said, confused.

"That money was going to be for Portland," she whined. "Do you know how much money it cost to relocate?"

"No," he said, answering the rhetorical question. "But I'm sure you do."

"It cost a lot. And I'm still paying for your ticket back, unless of course you decide to move out there with me." Her voice turned hopeful for a second and then declined back into a worried, nervous voice. "But you'd still have to go back to get your stuff, so I'd have to pay for a ticket either way."

He wanted to say not to bother paying for his ticket. He had gotten more out of coming along for the ride so far than she got out of having him as a road companion. But he was fearful of money too, especially because he dreaded the idea of going back to his old job. Still, he didn't want his worrier of a sister to worry anymore.

"Don't worry about my ticket," he said, reluctance in his voice.

"No," she said quickly. "I do what I say I'm going to do." He knew that she had a strong constitution but didn't know it was that strong.

Cosmo found an automobile repair shop that seemed decent enough by its customer reviews. He was glad it was on a quiet street instead of a busy highway, or as they called them here, freeways. The garage was a dark, cavernous place that took up almost an entire huge block. When they drove in, a thin man dressed in navy blue clothes greeted them.

"Can I help you?" he said, leaning in toward the car. He spoke with a thick accent, and when he opened his mouth, Cosmo could see several big metal fillings.

"I think the clutch is worn," Cosmo said, turning the car off and getting out.

"Let's take a look," the mechanic said. "You can wait in the office over there." He pointed to a window within the building, behind which Cosmo could see a Coke machine. Once they got inside, there was a worn blue sofa and an old end table that looked like one Cosmo had in his apartment. When he saw it, he wondered about his apartment. He asked his neighbor to keep an eye on it. Maybe he should shoot him an email.

As he opened his email, he saw another notice from the credit card company that his bill was due. In fact, soon it would be past due. He'd have to pay it tonight. He also saw another email from Dario, which said that the layoff was definitely over, and that they'd be resuming their jobs within a month. He wished he had never checked his email. He had had a whole day away from thoughts about his job and Philadelphia and real life. Now he felt trapped inside his head again.

"What's wrong?" Silvia said, flopping down on the sofa beside him, cup of coffee in hand. He must have had a worried look on his face for her to ask him what was wrong. He then noticed tension in his forehead and his jaws.

"Another email from Dario," he said in a somber voice. "The layoff is over."

"That's great," Silvia said, whose voice was anything but congratulatory. "You don't seem so happy about it."

He didn't have the energy to discuss how he felt with his sister. Even if he did, he wasn't sure what he felt besides confusion. He looked at Silvia waiting for some kind of answer though, so he felt that he had to say something.

"I think I was bored there." He surprised himself by telling her. She'd surely love hearing this.

"If you didn't come on this trip, you might have never known you were bored there," she said, implying that she was the one to credit for his newfound discovery. But she failed to address the problem, because she couldn't understand it. How could she understand? She had never stayed at a job for eight months, let alone eight years. She got a new job every other month; probably never even had health insurance unless she paid for it out of pocket; probably didn't even know what the word seniority meant. She might have even thought that his discovery of his boredom was a solution to the problem, instead of what it really was—the problem. He thought that explaining this to her was worth a shot.

"So I've been there for eight years. What would I do? Start over now? Come to Portland with you and serve coffee for a living?"

"You can always go back to Philly and get something else." He almost couldn't believe that she was suggesting something so practical. And he had thought of it. But it was more than that. It was more than getting a new job in the same old place. He wanted out of his old life. A part of him didn't want to tell her because he knew how she'd relish his desire for a clean slate, as he'd be seemingly following in her footsteps. But what choice did he have? Who else could he talk to besides himself? The mechanic. As Cosmo jokingly thought of telling the mechanic, he walked into the room.

"I got good news and bad news," he told them with a smile. "Which do you want first?"

"The bad," Silvia said.

"The bad news is you need a new clutch disc, which means a lot of labor cost, because we have to take the engine apart. The good news is we got a spare in one of our garages across town, and we can have it all done tomorrow."

"Tomorrow?" Silvia said, tensing her little body. "We have to get to Berkeley tonight. Or at least Santa Cruz." It seemed that her artificially created time constraints were even more important than the cost of the work, in which Cosmo was most interested. He wanted to ask, but he didn't want to make his sister any more nervous than she was already. But she had to find out eventually.

"So what will the cost be?" Cosmo asked.

"About eight hundred," the mechanic said. "You're welcome to get quotes from some other shops in the area though." Cosmo thought that the guy seemed honest and also thought that he'd only suggest going to other auto repair shops if he wasn't honest. He thought it sounded reasonable based on his limited car experience, but Silvia looked devastated. All the color had drained out of her face, and she looked even more tense and stiff than she did a minute ago. The mechanic, at seeing this, said that he could try to get it down to seven hundred.

"Thanks," Silvia said. "Is there any way it can be done tonight?" Apparently, she didn't want to go car repair shopping in Bakersfield. Cosmo was happy for that.

"Well, we close in less than an hour, and we still have to get the part. I've been here since six this morning. I can ask one of the other guys if they can stay late, but staying late can cost you." He slanted his lips and rubbed his grease-stained fingers together, signifying that the repair would be more costly than his quote of eight hundred.

"Let's just get a motel for the night and have him finish the job tomorrow," Cosmo said to Silvia.

"Can it be done early tomorrow, you think?" Silvia said to the mechanic with a pleading tone in her voice.

"Sure," the mechanic said. "I get in at six, so that shouldn't be a problem."

"Hey, since we have to leave the car here, you think we can get a lift to a motel nearby?" Cosmo said to the mechanic.

"I don't see why not," the mechanic said.

Cosmo looked for motels on his phone, while Silvia sat beside him looking glum and nervous at the same time. And despite her nervousness, she drank the stale coffee that was in the waiting room.

"This coffee's disgusting," she said taking a final sip. "I'm going to go get another cup. Want one?"

"No, thanks. Why are you getting another cup if it's so disgusting?" Cosmo said, puzzled.

"Because it's free," she said, getting up from the couch. "That's why." Was she turning into Frank, going for whatever was free? And was she now stooping to have trans-fat powdered crap in her coffee? Surely, there couldn't be real milk in the grimy automobile waiting room.

"I think I found a place," he said, staring into his phone, as Silvia re-entered the room with her second awful cup. "It's nearby, and it's cheap."

"That's good," she said in an expressionless, monotone voice. She sounded as if she couldn't care less.

"I'll call and make sure they have room," he said, ignoring her indifference.

After he called to reserve a room, he told Silvia that he'd go and see about getting a ride to the motel. She just nodded to him, eyes transfixed on the blank space in front of her. Her mind was undoubtedly too filled with car stuff for her to give a decent response. When he got back from finding a ride, she was still in the same position, and her face still had the same blank look on it, as if frozen in time.

"Some guy can give us a ride in a half hour," he said to her, not expecting anything in return.

"I think I'm going to sell that car as soon as I get to Portland," she said, a little less monotone than she had been previously.

"Oh, you're going to try to sell that piece of crap?" he said, waving his hand in the air.

"I can recoup some of my losses that way," she said, disregarding his put-down of her car. "Portland has a great public transportation system and lots of bike lanes. I'll get a bike." She seemed to be relieved with this thought, so Cosmo only agreed by nodding. "And it's not a piece of crap," she added.

The motel they found was like most of the others they had stayed in during the trip—plain, nondescript, and generic. It fit right in in Bakersfield, all of which was like a perfect grid with nothing but houses that all looked like each other and strip malls. Across the street from the motel was a strip mall, where they went out for Chinese food. As Cosmo sat, waiting for his shrimp fried rice, he thought about going back to his job. He saw himself sitting at his desk in his poncho, and this vision made him laugh to himself. The bright colorfulness of his poncho clashed horribly with the bland, drab gray and white office space, with his dull colleagues, and with the job itself. He was grateful when the food came to the table and put an abrupt end to his funny, but dark fantasy. But not long after they started eating, Silvia began with her travel plans for tomorrow, and at listening to her agenda, he suddenly lost his appetite. The idea of moving on was almost unbearable to him.

"Why do we have to be in such a fucking rush?" he said to Silvia. "I did you a favor by coming on this trip in the first place. The least you can do is let me enjoy it." He didn't like that he had reminded her twice of the fact that he was doing her a favor, but he had to say something in response to her rushing. She looked surprised at Cosmo's outburst, as if she didn't realize how much the rushing had been disturbing to him.

"I thought you'd want to get there so you can go back right away," she said. He said nothing because he didn't know what to say. He didn't know how he felt, besides lost, confused, and misdirected, as if he had gone the wrong way by a misleading road sign. So Silvia, being who she was, attempted to articulate his thoughts. "So you don't want to get there, and you don't want to go back? You want to just stay in between?"

He did want to stay in between, where he didn't have to worry about going back or starting new. In between sounded like the place to be. It sounded wonderful. He could happily stay in between, maybe picking up jobs here and there along the way to have money for food and lodging. He'd stay in between too, but reality kept crashing in like a drunken intruder, with its bills and rent and jobs. His sister was able to verbalize what he was feeling when he, himself, didn't even know what he was feeling. How could she be so understanding of his feeling unless she had felt it herself?

"How did you know?" he said, looking down at his plate of half-eaten food.

"Because I've been there." Just as he suspected. His sister's face turned sad, and she paused in eating her dinner of snow peas and tofu.

"Yeah, it's a shitty place to be," Cosmo said, sipping from his tea.

"Yeah," she said, still glum. "But there are worse places."

"Like what?"

"Like when you get to a place and you don't like it because it's not what you thought it would be, and you wish you could get out but you have no money so you're stuck, and you feel trapped like a rat." She said it all without a pause or a break, and it looked like just saying it drained her. Maybe she said it fast so she could get it over with. It did sound like an awful place, but not the same place that he was in.

"It doesn't really sound like the same place," he said. "I'm in this place of not wanting to go backward or forward. You always want to go forward. You're just sorry when you get there sometimes. I'm more in the place you were in when we were escaping one of Dad's rampages, and you didn't want Mom to stop driving. You didn't want to get to the motel, and you didn't want to go home." She got an expression on her face as if she understood the place that he was in. Cosmo felt grateful for the connection, and he went on in an effort to shed some light on her own dark and awful place.

"It doesn't make sense that you're in such a rush to get to wherever you're going. Maybe all that rushing is part of the problem. Maybe that's why you feel so awful when you get to a new place. Maybe you just need to slow down."

She looked down at her plate of food as if in deep contemplation, and then looked up at Cosmo. "Yeah, maybe you got something there. I think I'll give my friend in Santa Cruz a call, and we can stop by there tomorrow and then head up to Berkeley. That will slow the trip down." *It wouldn't,* thought Cosmo. It would just give them one more thing to do along the way. But maybe it was all he could expect from Silvia. He had to give her credit; she did hear him out, and she seemed to get something from his insight. And now she was back to thinking about his problems.

"What happens if you get to Portland and love it?" she asked.

He put his hands in the air and rolled his eyes back in his head as if to say that he didn't know what he'd do if this happened. This was exactly what he feared.

"Why not stay?"

"And serve coffee for a living?"

"What's so bad about that?" she said, looking right into his eyes. She had something there. It was a job, and it seemed like it would be more fun than the office job he had now.   "You don't think it would be crazy to give up my decent paying secure job for some minimum wage job with no benefits?"

"I think the only crazy thing is living a life you don't want." Cosmo never heard anything as clearly as he heard these words. It was almost as if the two of them were standing in a big cave, her words echoing in the air. He wished he could have listened to the echo of his sister's words a little longer, but she continued to talk.

"Have you thought about moving back, working, saving money, and then moving out?"

"And then I can just change my name to Silvia."

"Really, Cosmo. Why not?"

"Because I'm not like you. I don't like to uproot every few months. I like to stay settled. And besides, once I go back, it might be all too easy to get sucked back into my old life. Working my boring job, buying crap I don't need, being asleep again."

"Well, that sounds awful. Much worse than you moving to Portland. But you knew I'd say that. Hey, on another topic, let's see what our fortunes say." She smiled, going for one of the fortune cookies that had just arrived. He opened his to find a fortune that wasn't a fortune at all. And although it didn't tell of the future, it did warn him of his behavior, and in a way, it couldn't have been a more fitting warning: "Conquer your fears, or they will conquer you."

Chapter 10

The auto repair bill ended up being slightly more than seven hundred, and for this, Silvia was delighted. She was in a cheerful mood all through the morning. Cosmo wasn't feeling at all cheerful that morning. His sleep was interrupted with thoughts of going back to Philly, which was starting to seem inevitable. The part of him that was scared to get to Portland for fear of liking it and wanting to move there was growing fast, big, and furious, like one of the monstrous windmills that popped up around them after they got out of Bakersfield. The terrain felt more intrusive and less inviting than it had yesterday. The unfamiliarity looked weird instead of beautiful and interesting to him now, and made him feel like a stranger in a strange land. He felt alone and cold, despite the blazing sun. The dry angry winds offered nothing. No solace from his racing, scrambled thoughts that raced nowhere.

What if he got to Portland and liked it there, and liked Emily? Then he might not want to go back to Philadelphia. But if he stayed in Portland, what would he do for work? Should he cut out now, maybe fly back to Philadelphia at San Francisco to avoid any temptation in Portland? Should he move back to Philly and get back to his same job? If he did, would he get back into his old lifestyle, and if he did that, would he forget everything he had learned this week? Would all his new knowledge about life and how to live it be wiped from his mind? It might have to be wiped from his mind so that he could return to his dull, sleepwalking life. Would the divine part of him that had awakened after a long sleep go back to sleep? Was this the kind of crap that was constantly swirling around his sister's head? If it was, it was no wonder that she had spun her wheels and never got anywhere in her life. He looked at her driving her newly repaired car, and she appeared much more together than he felt. Of the two of them, she was usually the one scattered all over the place. It seemed that they had exchanged positions in some strange mental way.

"Cos," she said as she grabbed her plastic carry cup from its holder. "Can you look at the map and tell me what we need to look out for after Interstate 5?"

He grabbed the map from the side pocket of the car door, finding a highway leading into Santa Cruz. "Highway 152," he told her. It looked very narrow and windy from the map.

"Ah, that's a tough one. You don't get car sick, do you? Because if you do, you might want to drive."

"No," he said. At least, he could never recall getting car sick, but then again, he didn't have half the experience driving that Silvia had.

"Did you ever consider getting a truck driving license?" Part of him was serious and part of him was joking. She just looked at him with jaded eyes and duck lips. He assumed that the answer was 'No.'

The ride through Highway 152 did end up making Cosmo slightly sick, but he was actually grateful for the nausea as it diverted him from his problems and made him realize that he was making his dilemma bigger than it needed to be. Illness always did give him perspective. He was glad when they got into the town of Santa Cruz and he could get out of the car and put his feet on the ground. After doing so, his nausea dissipated instantly.

They stopped downtown in a small, tree-lined street filled with shops and cafés. Silvia parked in front of a restaurant that she claimed had the best home fries in the world. The place was busy, but there was a table available by the window where they'd be able to do some people watching. After they ordered, Silvia called her friend, Heather, who said that she'd meet them at the restaurant.

She came just as the server dropped off the food. She was dressed in ragged clothing and had matted hair, but she was pretty in a natural way with pale blue eyes that sparkled and glowing skin. She hugged Silvia and greeted Cosmo with a big, friendly hello.

"It's so great to see you, Heather," Silvia said, taking a bite of her tofu scramble. Heather had a smile on her face that made her look happy and uncomfortable at the same time.

"You too," Heather said, discomfort coming through her voice.

"Everything all right?" Silvia asked.

"I changed my name," Heather said. "So I don't go by Heather anymore. My name is Coyote."

Silvia looked slightly surprised, but mostly accepting. "Okay," she said as if she was curious to know why her friend had changed her name. Coyote must have sensed Silvia's curiosity, as she went on to explain why she changed her name.

"I went on a shamanic journey a few months ago and met my animal spirit; it was a coyote," she said with a slight giggle. "So now I'm Coyote."

"Cool," Silvia said, somewhat restrained. Cosmo could tell that his sister was lying and that she didn't find this name change cool at all. He suspected that she'd just avoid addressing her by her name for the rest of their visit.

"So where did you two meet?" Cosmo asked, trying to change the conversation away from the whole name thing.

"Art school," Coyote and Silvia said at the same time. Silvia seemed slightly more comfortable than she did a minute ago. Cosmo assumed it had something to do with the two girls' mutual history, and so he thought he'd indulge them in their memories of school.

"We met in a sculpture class," Silvia said. "Our sophomore year."

"I dropped shortly after," Coyote said as if she had no remorse at all for dropping out. "And I moved out here." Right after she said this, she excused herself for the bathroom. As soon as she left, Silvia let out a big sigh, as if she was hugely relieved.

"Oh, I'm not sure I want to stay for a long visit here, Cos," Silvia said, squinting her eyes. "She's weirding me out with that shamanic journey crap, and she stinks." She waved her hand back and forth in the air.

"Oh," Cosmo said, slightly dismissive. "She seems nice. And harmless."

"Yeah," she said, eating the last bit of her home fries. "Maybe I'm being judgmental. But I still want to make a short visit. I'll tell her we're rushed to get to Berkeley."

"How far is Berkeley?" Cosmo asked.

"Good question," Silvia said. "Can you look it up?"

"It's only an hour and a half away," Cosmo said, after about a minute of looking at his phone. "I guess we can say we need to make it up there for dinner." He ate the rest of his home fries and said, "Maybe we can all go for a walk by the beach or something and then split. It looks like a beautiful place, so we should at least enjoy it."

It was indeed beautiful, and it seemed as though the two girls got on all right. They chatted about old times as they all walked on a stone path the overlooked the ocean. In doing so, they gave Cosmo some time to himself. He had never seen the Pacific Ocean before this day. It looked much different that the Atlantic Ocean, just as Santa Cruz looked much different from any town on the Jersey Shore. There were mountains that framed the ocean; the occasional rock protruding out of the sea, some covered with seals, others with pelicans; trees with branches of deep green that swept dramatically toward the ocean, as if being pulled by the endless body of water.

But despite the vast differences between the Pacific Coast and the Jersey Shore, he couldn't help but compare the two places, and being here reminded Cosmo of his childhood beach days. For two consecutive summers, his family rented a place at the shore—a big, pink two-story box right on the boardwalk. Frank stayed inside the house most of the time because he didn't like the beach. He claimed to like the beach, but the few times he went, he'd complain continuously about the sun, the sand, the water, and the other people. Cosmo's mom and sisters would sit under the terrace of their rental that was within view of where Cosmo and Vince sat on the beach. He'd sit there all day under the yellow and green striped umbrella, while little Vince built sand castles beside him. As a child, he couldn't remember feeling asleep inside. He only remembered being alive and awake. But there had to have been a part of him that was numb, as he was so easily able to close out Frank when he was on a rampage. The others seemed to let him penetrate their skin. Maybe he really was sleeping through a lot of his childhood. Maybe that's when he learned to go numb, to sleep, to be dull.

Silvia snapped him out of his trance, asking him how he liked the Pacific Coast so far. Coyote was talking on the phone, so Silvia must have figured that this would be a good time to talk to her brother.

"It's nice," he said. "Different than the shore we grew up with."

"Yeah," she said, gazing out to the sea. "Out here, they never call it the shore. Or at least I never heard it called that out here."

"Mm," Cosmo said, eyes still set on the ocean.

"You sound interested," she said cynically.

"Sorry. I was just thinking about when we all used to go to the shore in the summer."

"Yeah. Those were some days. Sometimes I miss them, but then I remember always feeling on edge around Dad, and then I don't miss them."

"I don't miss feeling that way either."

"You never seemed like you felt uneasy." She turned to look at him. "Even when Dad was yelling right at you, you seemed like you could block him out. I was always jealous of how you could zone out like that. It really pissed him off too. I used to wish I could get his goat like that."

"Well, maybe you shouldn't have been wishing that," he said, turning to look right in her eyes.

"Huh?"

"The fact that you'd get anxious and scared showed you were alive. I'd go dead inside. I didn't realize then what a bad way that was to go."

"Why?"

"Habits are formed when you're young."

"So you think that's why you've become so dull and complacent in your adult life?" She smirked as if she thought there was humor in this statement.

"Yeah," he said decisively. "And I don't find it funny either." And then he smiled, which must have confused his sister. But he didn't smile because he found humor in his sad childhood story. He was just happy to be seeing his truth, and he couldn't help but smile for gaining this invaluable insight.

Meanwhile, Coyote finished with her phone call and rejoined them. Her eyes looked glazed, and she had a big smile plastered on her face.

"That was my boyfriend," she said.

"Oh yeah?" Cosmo said, trying to fake an interest. He thought that he had better think of something to ask her about her boyfriend. He imagined he also had some animal spirit name, maybe Crow or Zebra. "What's he up to today?"

"He's on call, but he had a minute so he called me."

"He works in the medical field I assume?" Silvia said cheerfully. "Good for you!"

"No. He's a psychic," Coyote said in complete seriousness.

Cosmo looked at Silvia, who looked like she was about to burst out in laughter. He forced himself to stop looking at her for fear that he'd have an outburst. He felt that he should clarify the story with Coyote too. Maybe there was something more to it. He once heard of a psychic that worked with cops to solve crimes. Maybe that was the case with this guy.

"He works on call?" Cosmo asked Coyote.

"You never know when someone might need a reading," Coyote said, still serious. So much for Cosmo's police theory.

"Mm," Silvia said, who to Cosmo's surprise, remained serious. She once told him that when she was trying to control her laughter outbursts, she'd think of something horrific and sad so that she wouldn't laugh. He could only imagine what she was thinking now. He tried to think of something terrible, but couldn't. He was still trying to wrap his head around Coyote's boyfriend's life.

Cosmo imagined that he lived in a tent on the beach or behind someone's house, that he rode his handmade bike to his psychic consultations, that he ate whatever organic scraps he could find, and that despite all of this, he was happier than a lot of other people leading conventional lives.

"He uses the Tarot," Coyote said, oblivious to the fact that they were both finding lots of humor in her boyfriend's strange career life.

"Our Uncle Vincent was big on the Tarot," Silvia said. "So was our grandma."

"Grandma Tucci?" Cosmo said with great curiosity. She couldn't have possibly been talking about Grandma Greco.

"Yeah," Silvia said, proud that she knew this curious fact about their Grandma.

"But she was a devout Catholic. How's that?"

"You know that the Tarot originated in Italy," Silvia said. "Maybe that has something to do with it."

"I never knew that about Grandma," Cosmo said, smiling into the air. He imagined his grandma laying out Tarot cards on her big old kitchen table.

"There're a lot of things about Grandma you don't know," Silvia said as if she had a great treasure of gold and was doling it out in the tiniest pieces.

"Your grandma must have been a cool lady," Coyote said.

Silvia smiled back at her and said, "Yeah, she was."

Their conversation ceased as they walked by a group of hippies gathered around a couple of bongo players. A woman danced around them, swaying her arms back and forth like an octopus with rhythm.

"So are you guys staying tonight?" Coyote asked. "You know you can totally crash at my place."

Cosmo looked to Silvia as if to say that whether or not they stayed the night was up to her. He wouldn't have minded staying in this lovely seaside town for a while, but he was sure his sister would want to be moving on. He was right.

"We promised our brother in Berkeley we'd be there tonight," Silvia lied.

"Oh, cool," Coyote said, seeming like she'd be fine with anything at all. "If you change your mind, the offer still stands."

"Thanks," Silvia said. "But like I said, we already made our plans with our brother. In fact, we'd better be on our way if we're going to be there by dinnertime."

"You should take the coast," Coyote said. "It's amazing."

"That's so out of the way though," Silvia said.

"I've never seen the Pacific Coast in my life," Cosmo said. "And I may not get another chance to see it."

"You're seeing it now," Silvia said looking out to the ocean.

"Well, I want to see more of it," Cosmo said, who so rarely demanded anything from anyone.

"You know we'll have to drive through San Francisco too?" Silvia said to Cosmo.

"I'll do all the driving then," Cosmo said, knowing that his sister couldn't resist such an offer.

"All right," Silvia said reluctantly.

They said goodbye to Coyote and headed back to the car.

"Ready to blow this Mr. Natural comic strip?" Cosmo said as soon as they got into the car.

"What's a Mr. Natural comic strip?" Silvia asked as she laughed at her brother's comment despite not understanding it. When he told her about Mr. Natural, she really laughed. They talked about Coyote and funnier yet, her on-call psychic boyfriend. Silvia expressed her guilt about talking about her friend several times throughout their mocking, although her guilt didn't stop her from continuing with her mockery. Cosmo imagined that they'd be joking about this day when they were both old and gray.

When their laughter calmed, Silvia sighed and said, "That was fun. I can't remember the last time I laughed so hard. I feel bad about talking about my friend and all, but it's just too fucking funny!"

Cosmo couldn't remember the last time that he heard his sister laugh so hard. He thought that she might laugh more if she wasn't so consumed with moving and doing all of the things that her constant moving required. She might live more too. She might slow down long enough to notice the world around her.

They drove up the coast with the ocean to the left of them and a combination of farms and tree-covered hills to the right of them. As the sun was setting, they came upon a small beach, and Cosmo pulled over so that they could watch the sun set.

"What are you doing?" Silvia asked as Cosmo pulled over.

"I'm pulling over so we can see the sunset," he said as he parked the car. He'd have told her ahead of time, but he knew that she'd probably give him a tough time. Besides, he might not have another golden opportunity like the one before him. They had driven on the coast highway for about an hour, and not all of the highway was right on the ocean. In some parts, the ocean and the road were separated by land.

"We don't have time to stop at for the sunset Cosmo," she said in her nervous voice. "We have to go all through San Francisco, and...."

"And what?" Cosmo interrupted.

Silvia looked stumped as if she was searching herself for the answer. But in a few seconds, she blurted out, "We have to get to Vince's."

"Is there a deadline to get there?" Cosmo said through curved lips.

"Well, no, but I'd like to get there some time tonight."

"And we will," Cosmo said getting out of the car. "It's only five thirty." Silvia followed, and together they crossed the road toward the shore. The beach was a small area, maybe only a couple of miles wide. They sat on the ground by the edge of the shoreline. The sun was about to make its descent, and it hung over the ocean, barely touching it. The sky was the palest shade of blue, almost white, and the air was filled with ocean dew. Silvia was sitting still, which was rare for her.

"Why is it so hard for you to sit still?" Cosmo said to Silvia.

"I don't know." But Cosmo was sure that she did know, but that she had pushed this knowledge away from her mind, and it was lost somewhere inside of herself.

"Dad can't stay still either. I'm not saying that you're anything like Dad, but maybe if you're not careful, you...."

"I'm never going to be like Dad," she interrupted him, probably knowing where he was going with his warning. "So don't worry about that." She was defensive and sounded almost as if she was trying to convince herself that she'd never end up like Frank. Cosmo, seeing her discomfort, changed the subject.

"The sun's about to go down," he said, turning his head away from his sister and toward the ocean. "We'd better keep our eyes on it. It's a quick show."

"It sure is," Silvia said, staring ahead. "The last time I saw an unobstructed view of the sunset was in Cape May. That was a while ago." Her voice had some remorse in it.

"You sound sad."

"I'm not sad. It's just that when I slow down to do things like this, I wish that I did them more often."

She stopped talking and he stayed silent. It sounded as though his sister might be coming to some conclusions about her life, and if that was the case, he didn't want to interrupt her train of thought. Besides, the sun was about one-tenth hidden behind the sea now, and he wanted to focus all of his attention on the sight before his eyes. Cars rolled by them, but they seemed distant, almost muted. His mind was mostly blank as the sun slid down, but one thought swirled around his head. He thought of how the sun had been setting every single day since the beginning of the world, and yet, a sunset was still a magical thing.

And just as it touched the water, a light went on inside Cosmo's head. He knew why Silvia couldn't stay still, and it was the same reason that he couldn't get moving. They were both scared. She was still running from one of Frank's rampages, and he was still trying to make himself invisible so that Frank wouldn't notice him. He wanted to feel angry with his dad, but he couldn't. He kept seeing his sad face, and in his mind, he remembered what Silvia had said to him about Frank once: "He can't help himself. He is who he is."

After the sun disappeared behind the sea, Silvia turned to him and said, "Thanks, Cosmo."

"For what?"

"For making me stop and see."

He was glad that she stopped long enough to see the sunset, and he felt a great sense of accomplishment in encouraging his sister to slow down long enough to see this glorious thing.

"You're a painter, Silv," he said getting up. "You need to stop and see the world whenever you can. If you don't start slowing down, all the beauty will keep zooming by you, and it won't look like anything at all." He almost surprised himself with the words that came out of his mouth. She was usually the profound one, imparting a lesson onto him. It felt good to be the wise one for a change.

———

They got to Berkeley around seven thirty. They pulled over as soon as they could after getting off at the exit for University Avenue, and Silvia called Vince.

"Hey, Vince," she said. "We're here!" She told him where they were and he navigated them to Telegraph Avenue.

Vince brought them to a pizza place that served the worst pizza Cosmo had ever had. The crust was big and airy and the sauce tasted like it came out of a jar. Still, he was starving, as he hadn't eaten since brunch in Santa Cruz, so he devoured two large slices before he even determined that the pizza he was eating was, in fact, lousy. Vince appeared happy with the pizza, as if he had forgotten in his very short time of living in California what real pizza tasted like. It had only been two months since he had left New Jersey, and already he seemed accustomed to his new place in the world.

He was much like Silvia in being adaptable and easily acclimating to new places.

Cosmo could never imagine himself moving to such a place so far away from home at Vince's age. He could barely imagine doing it now. He went to college only less than one hour from his home in New Jersey and that was tough for him. He was surprised to find himself feeling homesick. He missed Donna's cooking and the way she worried about him. He missed hanging out with Silvia and Vince. He even missed Frank in a strange way. He missed mocking him and getting under his skin.

Vince looked different from the last time Cosmo had seen him. He had seen him off at the airport with Donna. At that time, he looked scared and slightly lost, but being who he was, he tried to hide his fear and anxiety. He was probably more preoccupied with trying to keep Donna from crying, who in turn, was probably trying to be strong and unemotional for him. The bond between them was a tight one, which made Cosmo wonder long and hard why he'd want to go so far away for college. But Vince was destined for Berkeley, or a place like it, a place filled with young liberals like himself, energized by their hungry desire to make the world a better place. He claimed that not everyone at Berkeley was like him though, and some were just pretending. He called those types of people pretentious.

"There're a lot of pretentious types here," he said.

"Like who?" Cosmo asked as he opened the door leading out of the pizza place.

"Like people who say they're liberal but they're really rich, or people who act like they're into human rights but they own every Apple product made."

"That sounds more like hypocritical than pretentious," Silvia said.

"Well, yeah, it's hypocritical, but it's also pretentious," Vince said. It seemed as though he just really liked the word pretentious, and so he'd probably continue to use it every chance he got.

"Want to go for coffee?" Vince said as they walked by a café. "Cause this is a good place." He stopped in front of the café. It was a big, open space filled with students, many of whom had their laptops out in front of them. It reminded Cosmo of the café near his apartment in Philadelphia. He remembered going there with Silvia a week or so before their trip. Their outing at the café in

Philly seemed like it happened long ago. Cosmo was in a trance thinking about his neighborhood café, and his brother jarred him out.

"Cosmo," Vince said. "Where are you?"

"Oh, sorry, I was just thinking about something," Cosmo said. "Yeah, sure, let's go." He turned to walk into the café but was interrupted by Silvia.

"Can we go to a bookstore first?" she said. "I'm sure there's one a stone's throw away in this college town. I need to get a new journal. The café will be open for a while I'm sure. We can come back."

"Yeah," Vince said. "In fact, there's a bookstore right on the next block."

They all walked a block or so down the street, which was filled with cheap eateries and shops. They weren't fancy or high end, and they seemed to cater to students and hippies. Cosmo spotted a donut shop, a record store, a head shop, a hat store, and an Indian restaurant all in the same block. He wished that he could have walked more slowly down the street, but both Vince and Silvia walked very fast. He slowed down for a minute to peek into a shoe store and Silvia was quick to urge him along.

"C'mon, Cos," Silvia said with urgency. "The bookstore is going to close."

The bookstore was one large, bright, open floor, crammed with bookshelves. They all wandered in their own directions, and within a short time, Cosmo found himself in the spirituality section, where a copy of *The Eagle's Gift* by Carlos Castaneda stared him straight in the face. He associated Castaneda with his Uncle Vincent, whose apartment was filled with stringed instruments and books. Half of his books were Tolkien, and the other half were an eclectic mixture of spirituality and religion: St. Thomas Aquinas, Starhawk, Castaneda. He had started reading one of his uncle's Castaneda books when he was only thirteen, but grew bored with it quickly, and might have not even made it to the second chapter. But now when he read the back cover of this book, he thought it looked good and he decided to buy it.

He met Vince and Silvia at the register of the store. When he put his book down on the counter for purchase, Vince blurted out, "You're buying Castaneda?" He looked at his older brother, puzzled, and said, "Who are you? And what have you done with my brother?"

"Wiseass," Cosmo said, half-laughing.

"I think our big brother might be changing, Vince," Silvia said, smiling as they all exited the store.

"Yeah," Vince said to Silvia. "I think you might have something there."

They walked back to the café, which had grown more crowded in the past half an hour, and Cosmo felt lucky to find a tiny table in which they could all squeeze. Silvia and Vince got herbal tea and Cosmo got coffee, despite Silvia's warning that the caffeine would keep him awake. They also got a couple of oversized cookies to share. Silvia took her new journal out, opened the first page, and started drawing.

"Do you write anything in your journal, or just draw pictures?" Cosmo asked Silvia.

"I mostly draw in it, sometimes stuff I see, but it's usually ideas for paintings," she said. "That's why I always get blank pages. No lines."

"That's cool," Vince said, taking a bite of one of the cookies that equaled about half of the entire cookie.

"Yeah, I'm scared I'll forget my ideas if I don't get them down as I think of them."

"What are you drawing?" Vince asked.

"Well, if you must know," she said looking up from her journal to stare Vince in the eyes, "I'm drawing the sunset, but it won't look anything like any real sunset. It's just my take on it. I want to paint the sound it makes."

"That's crazy!" Vince said, big smile, eyes wide open. "It doesn't make any sound."

"I hear something in it," she said, smiling mysteriously as if she had a great secret and didn't want to divulge it to anyone. "And I want to paint the sound I hear."

"Silvia here is an artist," Cosmo said to Vince. "So she has a sixth sense." He turned to Silvia and said, "I'm just happy you stopped long enough to see it set."

"Yeah," she said to Cosmo. "Thanks for that. I've been rushing around like a nut, Vince, so thanks to Cosmo for making me notice it."

"I gather you guys saw the sunset coming up. You went up the coast then?"

"Yeah," Silvia said. "It was gorgeous and well worth the extra driving."

"Especially since I did all the driving," Cosmo added.

"Hey, you offered," Silvia joked. Cosmo made a goofy face, slanting his lips, curving his head down to the side, and opening his eyes wide. Silvia continued, "Anyway, I forgot how much I love to experience the sunset. It's so easy to get into rush mode, and once you're in it...." She stopped talking as if she had a loss for words. Both Cosmo and Vince looked at her with curiosity for what she had to say. She gazed at the ceiling, searching for words. Cosmo became tired of waiting and decided he'd finish the sentence for her. He had learned a thing or two about life this past week, so felt well-qualified to finish the sentence.

"Once you're in it, you can't get out, and it's like you're not really alive." Although he didn't rush around like Silvia, he went dead inside in another way, so he understood well enough to finish her thought.

"Yeah," Silvia said. "That's it." She and Cosmo needed no more words between them. They were practically telepathic with each other. But she must have felt a need to explain what they were both thinking to Vince.

"Vince, you're not there yet," she said to him. "When I was in college, I never got so caught up in shit that I lost perspective. I think it happens when you get out of school and reality hits you, and you have to worry about stuff like jobs and rent."

"You shouldn't assume it'll be that way for Vince because it was that way for you," Cosmo said to Silvia. "Maybe he'll never get that way." Cosmo realized that this was an unrealistic prediction, because he believed that everybody became asleep inside at some time during their lives. Silvia must have also recognized it.

"Everybody has to get out of touch with themselves at some point though," she said, drinking her last sip of tea. "The world takes people out of themselves. And they have to get out of themselves to live in the world."

"It doesn't have to happen to you either," Vince said to both of them. His young and innocent eyes shone with idealism. "I think it's the government that distracts us and diverts us from what's real, from all this self-intro-spection." Cosmo and Silvia waged bets ahead of time, on how long it would take Vince to mention something about the government, and with that comment, they sneakily stared at each other. Vince continued, "And it's the corporations—the ones that really run this country that are telling the government to distract us so we won't think about what's real, and we'll buy more shit we don't need made by slaves in China. And...." Although Vince may have had a point, Cosmo didn't feel like hearing it, and even more than not wanting to hear it, he wanted to get another cookie. He excused himself, and in doing so interrupted his brother, who didn't seem fazed at all by the interruption. He just continued with his rant, and when Cosmo returned to the table, he was talking about how the government created the recent bed bug scare as a distraction for the American public.

Silvia looked jaded and amused at the same time, but it was apparent that she wanted to change the subject. As soon as Cosmo sat down at the table, she said to him, "Why do you think you lost touch with yourself?" He thought she probably knew the answer already but wanted him to express it for himself. His brain struggled for words, but nothing came. He closed his eyes and saw himself as a teenager, at which time he decided that safety and boredom was the way to go.

"Fear," was the word that came out of his mouth. Simple, plain, and clear.

The next morning, Cosmo woke to a cloudless blue sky and was glad that he'd have a chance to see his little brother's college town in the light of a sunny day. With so many trees in Berkeley, he was reminded that it was fall. He had almost forgotten what time of year it was as he and Silvia passed through the desert. The town itself was flat and surrounded by hills. They walked through the campus, which was much different in appearance from the campus at the University of Penn, but still it was filled with that same kind of young, ambitious student energy as Penn, and it made Cosmo feel slightly nostalgic for his home. But not nostalgic enough to want to return.

Chapter 11

Saying goodbye to Vince wasn't as easy as Cosmo thought it would be. He tried to tell himself that he felt sad because he was being a bad big brother for leaving his younger brother to fend for himself. But Vince, like Silvia, didn't need an older sibling looking out for him. So it wasn't guilt that was making him sad. It was something else. He didn't know when he'd see Vince again, and he'd miss him. But it was something even more than that. Seeing Vince living so far from home at such a young age made him feel as if he was being left behind. Like Vince and Silvia had made the necessary separation from their family, and like they were moving on. And they were his younger siblings.

He wished that he had more time and space to feel sad, but as soon as they got in the car, he got a text from a manager in his department, Chris. The text told of a job that would be opening up, and it was one that Cosmo had had his eye on for a while. It would be a promotion, more money, more interesting work. He had to call Chris back immediately if he was interested, as interviews would start in a couple of days. Cosmo felt sick. He had to go back now. If he let this opportunity go, he might regret it for years to come. Going back from Portland would be tougher than going back from here. He should get a plane out of San Francisco and just end this journey while turning back wouldn't be so tough. Silvia would be fine for the rest of the trip. She could make it to Portland tonight, and she'd be with her friend, Emily. An imagined vision of Emily's face popped into his head. In this vision, she looked soft and pretty with eyes that understood everything. He forced the vision out of his head and concentrated on what he had to do to get back. He'd tell Silvia before the drive to Portland began. And just as he was ready to do so, other visions flooded his mind. He saw the eagle from the Grand Canyon. He saw Clay, Crazy Ted, the Truck

Stop Angel, and the cop who told him he was lucky to be alive. He saw Vince, Donna, Angie and Frank. He saw Silvia and him having one of their late night talks about life and death and eternity.

He stayed silent as Silvia drove to a nearby gas station. She was inside, paying the attendee for gas as he sat in the car, feeling more and more immobilized with confusion with each passing second. To make matters even worse, his phone rang, and it was Dario. He let it go to voicemail. He knew why he was calling. He was calling to tell him about the great job opportunity and that he had better hurry back.

He'd have his own windowless office big enough for him and a small desk. It would be private, so he wouldn't have to be sneaky about playing video games on his computer. He pictured it with a nice art museum print and a plant. With or without a painting and a plant, it didn't matter. His vision of the office looked more like a padded cell than a work space in his mind's eye. He'd have more money to buy more frivolous crap. He thought of all the people losing their shirts in these tough times, and he felt very small for frowning upon this great opportunity. He was becoming an unsatisfied brat like his sister. He had better get away from her too, or he'd be on her path of moving from place to place and continually starting over. She came back to the car and he asked if she needed him to pump the gas.

"Wow. You really are somewhere else. I just pumped the gas. Didn't you even notice?" she said with confused eyes.

"Oh, sorry," he said as if he was in some hypnotic trance.

The confusion that started in her eyes had spread to the rest of her face, as if understanding him was futile. So she started the car, driving out of the parking lot, but Cosmo stopped her.

"Wait, Silv," he said. "Can you pull over so we can talk?"

"All right," she said, still confused, but compliant. She pulled over to the side of the rest stop building, turned off the car, and looked at Cosmo as if waiting for an explanation.

"Would you mind if I go back from San Francisco?" He stared out the window as he spoke. He thought that looking into her eyes would make it more difficult for him to say what he needed to say. He didn't want to tell her about the job opportunity, maybe because he thought that if she knew, she'd insist that he go back. He secretly hoped that she'd insist that he come to Portland with her, so that he wouldn't have a decision to make. He knew that even if he did go to Portland with her, he might still have adequate time to prepare for his interview; but maybe it wouldn't be enough time, and then he'd screw up the interview and not have to take the job. He could have just rejected the offer to go to the interview, but that wouldn't look good. Besides, he'd be a careless fool to pass up the opportunity at hand.

He never understood confusion until now, how people could get so tripped up over deciding whether to take one course of action or another. He led a simple life, and whenever a choice presented itself to him, he just took the safe way. He would have kept on that same path too, had he not come on the trip that made him realize he had been unhappy taking the safe way. The feeling of gratefulness for this trip that he'd had at the Grand Canyon had faded, and now he felt only regret for coming on the journey. He should have stayed in his former, simple life. It was safe, and his brain never felt cluttered and messed up as it did now. He felt as if someone hijacked his brain, and he was fighting the thief with the little bit of strength he had left. It wasn't as though he was trying to fool himself. He didn't know at all what he wanted to do. So he hoped that Silvia would make up his mind for him. But no such luck.

"I understand," she said. "I just hope we can get a ticket for less than a million dollars. Maybe from Oakland. Of course, we'll have to do standby." She put her head down and put on her worried face as she planned on how to get him back to Philadelphia immediately.

This was the last response he expected from his impractical sister. Now his only hope was that the flight would be too expensive to go back right away, or that he wouldn't get in on a flight on standby. If they went to the airport and he did get into a flight on standby, he'd have to go. There'd be no turning back. He'd have to go forward to his backward existence. How he wished Silvia could have had a different response. He thought that she needed him to go to Portland with her. He now saw that she didn't need him at all. She only wanted him to go with her. Why did her fierce independence have to come out now? Maybe he could talk her into needing him. She had told him about the way that she'd crash soon after she got to a new place. Maybe with her brother there with her in her new place, she wouldn't crash. He could at least remind her of what she had told him.

"Are you sure you won't want me there with you in Portland? Just while you get settled? I'm thinking about what you told me in the Chinese restaurant. About how you crash every time you get to a new place."

"Yeah, of course I do. But your job is more important. I mean, that's your livelihood, and I don't want to interfere with that." She was being more selfless than her usual self-involved, twenty-four year old self. Why now? Maybe all that slowing down stuff had something to do with it. Maybe she was more in touch with herself now (thanks to him), and now she didn't need him so much. Damn!

Then he considered another option for her sudden, apparent selflessness. She knew him better than anyone did. So maybe she knew that he didn't want to go back, but that his pragmatic, responsible, scared self was pushing him in that direction. Surely, she would want him to admit this truth to her and to himself. But something in him couldn't give his little sister the satisfaction of admitting his confusion to her. He knew that she always thought of him as the stable one in the family, as the one who had his feet on the ground. She might have been able to talk a good game of wisdom, but she couldn't live her life. He didn't want to go over to her side and become someone who was always searching, never satisfied with what life gave him. Admitting to his confusion would be enough to join her, and once his words hit the air, the thoughts inside his head would become his reality. Those words, once spoken, would become part of his history as a human being. He'd lose who he was and become a searcher like his sister and like all of the other searchers who never find what they're after.

"All right," he said. "Should we go to the Oakland airport first then? See what's up there?" He hoped that she'd be reluctant to go to the airport now that he pretended that he wanted to go back to Philly, but this wasn't the case.

"Yeah. Can you get me directions on your phone?" she asked him. "We have to get there quick though, because I still want to make it to Portland by tonight."

"Isn't that a long way from here?"

"Yeah," she said. "But I'll just drink lots of coffee. It doesn't matter if I get there in the middle of the night. I'm staying with Emily, and she doesn't care."

Cosmo's imagined vision of Emily came into his head again, and she looked prettier than ever. He sunk down further. He wondered if his sadness showed to Silvia. She was so damn perceptive of him, so she probably knew and was faking this whole thing just to get him to admit his confusion. He had too much pride to let himself slip, so he went along with the show and looked up the directions to the Oakland airport on his phone. He had hoped that it was a long way from where they were so Silvia had time to change her tune and encourage him to come with her to Portland, but upon looking up the directions, he saw that it was only about fifteen minutes away. He didn't want to make her drive there in hopes of there not being any standby opportunities for flights going to Philly, but admitting his confusion to her wasn't something he could imagine doing. So he dictated the directions to her as he desperately hoped for a traffic jam.

"Hey, I just thought of something," she said as she was driving. "If there aren't any standby opportunities at the airport today, you can stay at Vince's and try for tomorrow." She seemed so proud of this new idea that made Cosmo feel more hopeless than ever. He felt the kind of sadness inside that he hadn't felt in years. The kind that made him want to hide underground and never come out. For some reason, Angie's face came to his mind. He saw her in her high school years when she had gone to the hospital one night for swallowing too many pills. He remembered feeling angry with her at the time. How could his beautiful, popular sister who Frank so strongly favored have done something like this? He felt an understanding for her that he never knew before this time. How could he have been such a bastard of a brother to her for all these years? It wasn't her fault that she was Frank's favorite and that he was his father's least favorite. He had to call her as soon as he could. But there were matters more urgent now.

"Where do I go now?" Silvia said urgently, prompting Cosmo to continue with his directions.

He looked down at his phone and said, "Take the next exit up here." His voice was so deep and somber that it almost felt as if it didn't belong to him.

"Are you all right, Cos?" Silvia said. Cosmo was starting to get angry with her, as he assumed that she was egging him on and she knew that he didn't want to go back, that he was hoping she'd urge him to come with her to Portland.

"I'm fine," he lied.

"No, you're not," she said right back.

"Well, all right," he said finally with a combination of relief and exhaustion. "I'm not fine! I'm totally fucked up! Are you happy now?"

"Huh?" Silvia said, glancing at him with shock. Maybe she wasn't playing any head games all this time and he had just suspected her of doing so because it was something to do. It was easier to feel some superficial anger at his sister than all the deep, dark, messy, alien stuff inside of him.

"I'm pulling over," Silvia said. Cosmo couldn't object. He was certainly in no rush to get to the airport. She pulled over at the parking lot of a Denny's and turned off the car, waiting for Cosmo to begin talking. He couldn't verbalize the jumbled up mess inside his head, so he sat silently. After about a minute of silence, they both started to talk, and their words blurred together.

Cosmo started to say "I don't know..." and at the same time, Silvia said, "So you don't want to..." Silvia then turned to her brother and waited for him to talk.

"I don't know what I want, and it's a really weird feeling for me, because I've never felt it before."

"I think it's called confusion."

"Yeah, confusion," Cosmo agreed. "I always thought confused people were idiots who made their lives harder than they needed to be. Guess I'm one of those idiots now."

"I don't think that at all. I think that life is confusing, and that the confusion you're feeling just shows you're alive."

These words resonated with Cosmo. He did feel more alive this week than he had in years, so maybe the confusion went with feeling of being alive.

"Why do you think being alive and being confused go together?"

"You're confused because you're questioning your life, and you're questioning your life because life is confusing." She used circular logic but she wasn't being illogical, and he nodded his head in agreement.

"I think that you know what you want though," she said. "And you're just fighting what you know." These last words went deep within Cosmo to a place where there was no room for lies or deception—where there could be only truth. He knew what he wanted and that was to keep going forward to Portland, which had become much more than a place to him. In going forward, he was going forward inside himself. He was continuing on the internal journey that he had begun when the truck wiped them off the road. Philadelphia had also grown to become more than a place inside of his head. Going there meant going backward, going back to his old way of being in the world. It meant feeling stale and tired and old and dead.

He took his phone out and keyed in the number for his old place of work, which prompted Silvia to ask him whom he was calling. "I'm calling my old boss to tell him I won't be back in time for the interview," he answered. Silvia made a smile so big that it took over her entire face. She started the car and said, "Portland, here we come!"

Chapter 12

Highway five was straight and flat until they got near Mount Shasta, where large mountains rose up on the sides of the highway. The road itself became steep, rising and falling and wrapping around the mountains. The change in altitude made Cosmo's head feel like a balloon, and he couldn't hear right, but eventually his ears popped, his head felt less swollen and more clear than ever. With his head feeling so clear, he remembered that he wanted to call Angie. He asked Silvia to stop at the next rest stop. They stopped at a rest area surrounded by trees that had a bathroom and some park benches. This was as good a place as any to make his call. He didn't have her number but was sure that Silvia would have it. He was right. When he asked her for Angie's number, she smiled deviously, as if it was because of her that he wanted to call Angie. And although Silvia had a lot to do with his wanting to call her, it was something that he was doing of his own volition. Silvia said that she'd wait by the car while he sat on top a picnic table to make his call.

Angie's phone rang several times, and Cosmo suspected she wouldn't answer the call. Maybe she knew it was him by the Philadelphia area code, and she didn't want to deal with him. He couldn't blame her. He was ready to leave a message when she answered.

"Mom?" she said in a puzzled voice. She must have assumed it was Donna, as he and his mom lived in the same city and shared the same area code. Maybe she only answered because she guessed it was Donna.

"Hey, Angie," he said. "It's Cosmo." The tone of his voice was sad and remorseful.

"Hey, Cosmo," Angie said with surprise, her greeting sounding more like a question than a statement. He hoped that she'd say more, but she didn't. He had never called her, so she might have been so shocked to get a call from him that she was speechless.

"How's it going?" he said. It was the only thing he could think to say. It was a conversation starter though, and his sister was good at conversations.

"Good," she said. "Not so different than when I talked to you last." Cosmo couldn't wrap his head around the fact that it was only a week ago when they last talked. He had even forgotten about it until she reminded him. When he talked to her at Frank's house, he had been forced and had nothing to say to her. Now he had something to say. He just didn't know how to say it.

"Yeah, twice in one week," he said forcing a laugh.

"Yeah," she said, her voice still sounded puzzled. "Why is that? I mean, I haven't heard from you for years. So I have to say, I'm a little surprised." She certainly had a right to be, and he knew now that he couldn't stall with what he had to say for another second longer. Silvia was waiting for him, and they had to make it to Portland some time tonight or at least by the early morning hours of tomorrow.

"Well, Silvia and I have to get back on the road so I don't have long to talk," he paused for a few seconds, gathering strength for what he was about to say. "I just wanted to say sorry for beheading your favorite Barbie doll, and for all the times I called you a stupid girl, and for not accepting the honor of being Isabella's godfather. And well, I'm just sorry for being such a jerk of a brother to you all these years." He left it at that. He could have said more in an effort to explain his past actions or to try to justify his being a jerk, but there was no reason for it. It would just be a lot of extraneous words, and life was too short for that sort of thing.

"Wow," she said sounding a bit shocked. "I wasn't expecting that." He heard something besides shock in her voice. He could hear her happiness coming through the phone. As far apart and as different as they were, they were still brother and sister, and they could still had a connection, and could hear each other even when the other was silent. He heard her crying, but he could tell that she wasn't crying out of sadness. They were happy tears. "Thank you, Cosmo," she said through her tears. And then she added, "I love you."

These were easy words for Angie. Cosmo had heard her say them to every member of their family at least once. He had never said it to anyone that he could remember. It didn't mean that he didn't feel love for people. He just couldn't speak those words so freely. He had written them in a letter to Donna once, and once to a girlfriend he'd had years ago. When he considered the great infrequency in which he had conveyed those words to the people in his life, he realized that this was one more way in which he had safely shut himself off to the world. What if he and Silvia had died a week ago? What if Angie and everyone he loved died? He would have one more regret to stuff in his big bag of regrets? It might have been the biggest of all. He couldn't hold himself in any longer.

"I love you too," he said. And with those words, the many years of dirty looks, cruel remarks and bad wishes that they had both had for each other had faded into the air. Just at that second, he looked at Silvia, who looked nervous, undoubtedly about the passing of time. Cosmo was sure though that despite her nervousness, she didn't want to interrupt the exchange between her brother and sister.

It wouldn't be easy to say goodbye to Angie, who was still crying. It wouldn't be easy to end the conversation that felt like the first real exchange between him and his sister. But he knew there'd be more to come, and he also knew that there'd be more time to share with his adorable, little niece, Isabella. He quickly imagined himself doing magic tricks for the girl, buying her birthday gifts, and seeing her grow up. And just as he thought of Isabella, he heard her call out for Angie in the background.

"Mama," she said in her high-pitched voice.

"Come here, Isabella," Angie said. "I want you to say hi to your Uncle Cosmo." Angie put her on and she said, "Hello, Uncle Coso."

"Hello, Isabella!" Cosmo said, half-laughing over his niece's mispronunciation of his name.

Angie got back on the phone and said, "I know you guys have to get going. Give my love to Silvia, and safe travels."

———

As they drove on to Portland, the tangled feelings inside of Cosmo began to straighten. The emptiness filled up, and by the time they got there, he almost forgot how lousy he had felt earlier that very same day. He even forgot why he felt that way. He knew it was about his indecision about going back to Philadelphia, but couldn't remember why he agonized so much over the decision. He saw the true smallness and insignificance of this decision in the whole scheme of things. He saw that whether he decided to do one thing or another, his life would still go on, and the world would continue on its path. It wouldn't shake or tremble in the slightest. The sun would set every night. Birds would sing songs in the morning. Stars would shine in the nighttime sky. Why did something that was so big to him just a few hours earlier shrink so much to its appropriate size? It could have had something to do with his call to Angie and his reclaiming his perspective of what was important in life. He knew that he'd lose it again though. He knew that the world would continue to take him out of himself, as Silvia had said. But it was only right that he should enjoy the feeling of well-being while it was there for him to enjoy.

As they passed a microbrewery, he suggested that they go in for a beer. "We can have Emily meet us there," he told Silvia as he pulled over to park the car. A part of him was nervous about meeting Emily, and he thought it would be easier if she could meet them at the bar rather than crashing at her house. Besides, they had made better time than they expected, as they only made two quick stops the whole way. It was only nine o'clock, so they had time to stop.

"Since when do you want to have a beer, Cosmo?" Silvia said with worried eyes. "First, you wanted the margarita in New Mexico, and now you want a beer. You know men are more likely than women to inherit the alcoholic gene."

"I can assure you that I'll never be a drunk like Dad," he said, getting out of the car. "And speaking of Dad, you sound just like him, talking about genes."

"It's true," she said, disregarding his comparison of her to Frank. "I heard that somewhere."

"I think if I was going to be an alcoholic, I would have done it by now. I'll be twenty-nine next month."

"It's never too late to fuck up your life," she said, smirking.

"I'll consider that," he said, opening the door to the bar.

"I'll call Emily and see if she can meet us here."

"Sounds good. What do you want to drink?"

"I don't know," Silvia said, looking around the bar as if she had no idea what to order. "I guess some kind of beer."

He looked back at her with a cynical stare and said, "Oh, really?"

"Is there any such thing as a sweet beer? I think beer tastes like liquid ear wax for the most part."

"You're so gross," Cosmo said, half laughing. "And how do you know what ear wax taste like anyway?"

She didn't answer. She just waved her hand in the air, slanted her lips, and walked away, presumably to a less noisy place to make her phone call. Cosmo went to the bar and asked the bartender for a sampler and a Lambic. Silvia finished her call and came back to the bar in time for the arrival of their drinks, and they toasted to their safe arrival to Portland.

"Here's to making it here in one piece," Silvia said, awkwardly raising her glass as if it was the first toast she'd ever made in her life. She hadn't touched the glass to her lips when she thought of something else. "And here's to you coming all the way, Cos!"

Cosmo smiled and added, "And here's to never becoming an alcoholic!" They both laughed as they clashed glasses, and Silvia announced that Emily was coming to meet them shortly.

"Cool," Cosmo said, trying to act casual.

"You guys remind me so much of each other," Silvia said. "I'm excited for you to meet."

Cosmo gave a smile and drank down half of his beer. He tried to hide his nervousness, but Silvia saw right through it.

"Are you nervous?" she said, delight in her eyes. "You shouldn't be. Emily is such an easy-going person."

And she was. When she came up to the bar, Cosmo felt instantly at ease. She radiated warmth and comfort. She hugged Silvia and smiled big at Cosmo, revealing her straight and shiny teeth. She had hazel eyes that sparkled with the rest of her. Her hair was made of dirty blond curls that scattered around her heart-shaped face and fell onto her neck. Cosmo thought of what Silvia told her about Emily being a geek. She didn't look at all like a geek. But she seemed to have a taste for geek culture, which he could see right away.

"We should go to this cool arcade right around the corner," she said. "They have these old pinball machines from the seventies and old Pac-Man machines from the eighties. It's so cool!" She looked to be older than Silvia and possibly even a bit older than Cosmo, but she was almost like a teenager in her mannerisms and her way of speaking.

"Want to have a drink here first and then we'll go?" Silvia said excitedly as she took a sip of her drink.

"Yeah," Cosmo said to Emily. "What are you drinking?"

"Oh," Emily said, pursing her lips and putting her hand on top of her head. "I'll have an oatmeal stout."

After Cosmo got the beer, she thanked him graciously, as if he had given her something more than a drink. He wasn't used to people being so gracious to him. He tried to think of some conversation to make, but his mind was tired from his anxiety-filled day and from his nervousness over meeting Emily. He was glad and grateful she and Silvia had no shortage of conversation so he could relax and pretend to be interested in their conversation while he stared at Emily's face. Whatever they were saying to each other sounded blurry and distant to him.

"You got the sampler," Emily said to Cosmo, trying to drag him into their conversation.

"Yeah," he said making a closed-lip smile, nodding. He tried to think of something smart to say but the only thing he came up with was, "How's your beer?"

"Oh, it's great," she said in a bubbly, spirited way. Her voice sounded higher than what he heard through Silvia's phone, but she may have been making it higher so he could hear her over the loud music.

His mind went blank again. This was rare for him. He could always think of something to say. He was relieved when Silvia, probably seeing him at a loss for words, started up a conversation about how she and Emily had met.

"So we worked in the same bookstore in Tucson," Silvia said. "Emily showed me the ropes there." Emily gave a slight laugh.

"Are you from Tucson?" Cosmo asked.

"Unfortunately," she said almost as if she was embarrassed for being from this place.

"What do you mean?" Cosmo asked. "You don't like it much?"

"Not so much," Emily said. "I can't stand the summers. They're brutal. The rest of my family seems to do all right there though. They're still there. At least part of my family."

"It must be pretty though, I bet," Cosmo said.

"Oh it is," she said.

"They have a great program in astronomy at the university there," he said, remembering a guy he knew from Penn that went on to graduate school there.

Emily stared back at Cosmo as if she was slightly confused, but Silvia explained, "Cosmo studied astronomy in college."

"Really?" Emily said. "You must be smart. I always think that people who are good in science are smart. All that stuff is beyond me." She waved her hand in the air. Her hands looked strong and artistic at the same time, and her long, thin fingers flowed through the air as if they were dancing. Cosmo was too busy looking at her to respond to her comment, so Silvia spoke for him once more.

"Yeah, he's the brains in the family," she said looking at her brother, prompting him to speak. By the look on her face, Cosmo could almost hear her saying, "Fucking say something, you dork!"

"Well," he said looking down. "I don't know about that. I just like astronomy. I guess because there's so much mystery out there." Cosmo couldn't recall ever articulating what it was that he liked about astronomy.

Emily looked at him endearingly and said, "That's so cool! I love it." She was so full of life and exuberance.

"Thanks," Cosmo said. "I only stayed in school for a couple of years. I dropped before my third year."

"Do you ever think of going back?" Emily asked in an encouraging tone.

Before this week, he had not thought about returning to school. In fact, before this past week, he had never felt regret for dropping out. But now the thought of returning to school produced a vision in his mind that was bright and made him feel happy and light. Learning was the thing that made him feel alive. It was the thing that he was put here to do. When he thought of going back to school earlier that week, he quickly dismissed the idea with the assumption that it was too late and that he was too old. That was a stupid thing to think. It wasn't as if he was going back to school to be a circus performer or something else that necessitated his being young. Why hadn't he considered this before? Maybe because his mind stayed so straight and narrow before. It never strayed into the lands of his many possible paths in life.

"I do think about going back," he said, as if proud of his new realization. Silvia looked at him admiringly and Emily seemed happy with his answer too.

"I do too," she said. "I studied English literature in college, so I pretty much have to go back for something. I'm not sure what though." Her bubbly tone of voice went flat.

"Maybe you can go back to school for something that interests you. What do you like to do?" he asked her, finishing off one of his small glasses of beer.

She looked up at the ceiling and said, "I like to read books, play video games, ride my bike, go out for coffee, listen to music, watch movies, and a bunch of other stuff that can't make me any money." She laughed and took a big gulp of her beer. Of course, she named things that he also liked doing. He was surprised that stargazing wasn't one of the things she mentioned, but he felt sure that if this activity was suggested to her, she'd be all for it. He could see Silvia out of the corner of his eye with a proud, self-congratulatory, smug face, probably at having discovered her newfound skill of matchmaking. He tried not to focus on Silvia so he could say something thoughtful and smart to Emily.

"I found a way to make money, and I don't even have a degree. I do I.T." Emily smiled at him, her encouraging expression prompting him to tell her more.

"It was something I kind of fell into after dropping out. How convenient, right?" He couldn't think of any more to say, perhaps because he was down on his job. So he asked what Emily did for a job.

"I work at Powell's," she said. Cosmo looked back at her as if perplexed, and so she explained more. "It's a big, independent bookstore in town. One of the last standing in this country of ours." She took a last sip of her beer and added, "I feel lucky to have a job. My dad just got laid-off after twenty-five years."

"Sometimes those layoffs end," Cosmo said, trying to make Emily smile again. It worked. She smiled and then excused herself for the restroom. As soon as she left, Silvia turned to her brother, smiled, and said, "Isn't she great?" And without giving him a chance to answer, she added, "I just knew you guys would hit it off." Cosmo laughed and looked down. He felt happy and confused at the same time and wondered if it showed in his face. Of course, if his confusion showed in the slightest, his little sister would notice it. She did.

"What's wrong?" she said as if frustrated with her brother.

"Well, you know I have to go back eventually." He said this more like a question than a statement because it felt more like a question. He only wished he had someone, beside himself, to ask this question.

"You don't have to, Cosmo," Silvia said, as if pleading. "Stay here with me, and together we'll start a new life, away from our screwed up family. Away from who we were back there." She was rarely so melodramatic, but when she was, she sounded as though she should be standing on a podium somewhere with lost souls listening to her every word, as if her words both shattered and mended their worlds at the same time.

Still, her words were not enough to convince Cosmo, who was still torn about whether to go back to his job. He knew that he didn't want to take the promotion because he'd probably feel committed to staying, so he was happy that he had called Chris to tell him he wouldn't be there for the interview. But maybe going back to his old job temporarily wouldn't be so bad. Maybe he was lucky to have a job. Just as he was about to say something, Silvia said. "Oh, here she comes" with a sense of warning in her voice.

"You guys want to go to the bar with the arcade machines?" Emily asked.

"Sure," Cosmo said, getting up. The three of them walked out into the light drizzling rain. People rode bikes and skateboards as if it were not raining. When Silvia said she wished that she had an umbrella, Emily turned and looked at her as if she said something offensive.

"You better get used to the rain without an umbrella, Silv," Emily warned. "Or else you'll be pegged as a tourist. You don't really need one anyway. It's light rain, and if you're worried about your hair getting big, just wear a hat." She put her hand in her bag and dug out a red cap, putting it on her head. The hat didn't go too well with the rest of her outfit, which consisted of a flower-patterned skirt and a pair of boots, but she didn't seem to care, and this made her all the more charming to Cosmo.

As they walked to the arcade, Cosmo couldn't stop looking everywhere. They passed by old, brick buildings with marquee signs, free flowing water fountains, Philadelphia lampposts, and public sculptures, one of which was a triangular-shaped tower of antique kids' bikes stuck together. Cosmo had never seen anything quite like it. Silvia stopped to stare at it. Cosmo felt proud of his sister for stopping and noticing, and he felt proud of himself for having something to do with her pausing. This was who she was as a child, always looking at the world with open eyes, ready to capture everything around her so her surroundings could become a part of her and so that she could re-express what she saw through her art.

The place with the old video games was half arcade and half bar. It was a dark, two-story place with a small bar and every available space filled with big old, clunky video game machines. The upper level had the dated pinball machines and the first floor had mostly machines from the eighties, like Miss Pac-Man. This seemed to be Emily's favorite, as it was the machine she ran toward. She tied her hair back in a knot on the top of her head and intently focused on eating the miniature digital fruit. With her hair away from her face, Cosmo could see her high cheekbones and the way that her eyebrows were slightly darker than the hair on her head. The noise of the place was almost assaulting because he had grown so used to calming, natural sounds, like the desert wind, the birds, and the ocean waves. But when he looked at her face, the noise sounded like no more than a distant hum.

"Oh, yay for me!" Emily said as she jumped up and down. She had reached her high score. He remembered the night that he reached his high score at Alien Storm. He was thirteen, and his family had rented a house in Ocean City, where they had blue laws, which required the arcades to close down on Sundays. He and his friend waited up until midnight that night for the arcades to re-open. He could still recall the feeling of excitement at seeing his high score on the screen. He didn't jump up and down and scream "Oh, yay for me!" but probably would have had he been a girl.

Emily was a woman, but she still had a girlish quality to her. Not just in the way that she jumped up and down at getting her high score, but the way that she moved through the world with a type of carefree spontaneity that only children show. As if she was freer than other adults were; or, at least, she appeared that way to Cosmo.

"I'm hungry," she said suddenly. "Let's get nachos."

Cosmo liked this suggestion although Silvia looked anything but pleased with the idea of nachos.

"You guys can eat them," Silvia said. "I'm not that hungry."

"Are you sure?" Cosmo asked Silvia out of obligation. "We can get something else." He hoped that she'd just insist that they get the nachos, and to his relief, she did. Silvia also may have wanted to give the two of them some time alone, as when the nachos came, she said that she wanted to go play on the pinball machines upstairs.

"How long have you lived here?" Cosmo asked Emily.

"Only a couple of years now," she said, dipping into the nachos. "I moved up with a boyfriend, but we're not together anymore." Cosmo was glad for that, but did his best to conceal his feelings.

"And the bookstore?" he asked.

"Oh, I got the job shortly after I moved." She took a very brief pause and then asked, "And you live in Philadelphia?" Cosmo was hoping it wouldn't come up, but he also knew that he'd eventually have to talk about his current life situation. He slanted his lips and put both of his hands in the air, and said, "Technically. Yeah, I live and work in Philadelphia. But there's a part of me that doesn't want to go back. Maybe I've been on the road too long, but it's only been a week, so I guess I shouldn't use that excuse."

"What do you mean by excuse?" she said with an inviting expression in her eyes, as if she knew he needed to clarify his thoughts. Cosmo searched himself but found nothing in terms of an answer, so he said nothing. She seemed to want to help him, so she continued. "What I meant to say is that maybe you shouldn't think in terms of excuses for doing what you want to do."

Cosmo lifted his brows, prompting her to continue. "I mean, you should be able to do what you want to do, as long as you're not hurting anybody." Before the trip, he would have dismissed thoughts of doing what he wanted, calling them naive and unrealistic, but he could no longer fool himself into living a life he didn't want.

"Until now, I didn't know I didn't want it," he told her, opening his eyes wide. "Crazy, huh?"

"No," she said in a self-assured tone. "Not crazy at all. Sometimes it takes a while to know what you want. I still haven't figured it out." She picked up a chip and studied it as if it might contain the answer, and then came back with, "Hey, at least I'm having a good time though." She had a point.

"You like working at the bookstore then?"

"Sure, but I can't see me doing that when I'm old. I need to get some kind of skill like you have."

"I'm not sure I want to be sitting in front of a computer the rest of my life either."

"If you could do anything, what would it be? I mean, imagine money, job prospects, and all those practical considerations didn't matter."

Cosmo didn't have to look too hard within himself to find the answer to this question. And as soon as she finished talking, he got a picture of a nighttime, star-filled sky. "I'd be an astronomer." He had never felt so sure about anything. There was no confusion in him, and it felt good to have some clarity about something for the first time in what felt like forever, but had, in actuality, only been about a week.

"That's incredible," she said in response to his desire to be an astronomer. She opened her eyes wide, rested her chin, and looked at Cosmo as if he was her hero. He wasn't used to being looked at that way. He couldn't remember anyone ever looking at him that way. He couldn't recall anyone using the word incredible to describe him or his aspirations. He could tell that she wanted him to say more. While he did want to elaborate, he also wanted to know her dream.

"What about you? What would you do if money and all that practical stuff was irrelevant?" Cosmo was sure that she probably had an answer prepared. She was, after all, Silvia's friend, and he assumed that she wouldn't have posed the question to him had she not given it considerable thought herself. But she didn't have a definitive answer.

"I don't know," she said, not seeming at all disturbed about not knowing. "I like to do so many things, but nothing that I can make a living at. "

"Well, I probably can't make a living being an astronomer. I think you forgot what the question was."

"Oh yeah," she said as if she didn't know that she lost sight of the question. She looked up at the ceiling and put her hand on top of her head to take the knot out of her hair, letting her soft curls fall down. She said, "I would write comics." She laughed and turned her head to the side and went on, "I started making comic strips when I was in fifth grade." Cosmo wondered if they had been living parallel lives from across the country as he, too, used to make comic strips as a boy.

"Wow! I used to make comics too. I made one with a hero named Captain Quasar from the Starburst Galaxy," he said as he took grabbed a handful of chips. "His superpower was that he could make himself so super bright that he could blind villains."

"That's so cool," she said giving him that hero look again.

"Thanks. Tell me about yours."

Emily's face lit up so much that it almost looked glow-in-the-dark. "I made a girl character named Lulu. She wore a red dress and had black hair, and she was feisty and little but big in her own way. She was like Silvia!" she said excitedly, as if she had just realized, at this second, that her comic book character was like Silvia.

"That's awesome," Cosmo said, kicking himself right after for not saying something more original. He didn't even like the word awesome. But Emily didn't seem to be anything but flattered and touched by his comment, as she smiled and continued.

"Well, I just kept making them. And I kept adding characters. And the main character Lulu became more and more real. And I kept at it until...." She stopped talking and looked down. The smile on her face faded and Cosmo became curious as to the cause of her sudden unhappiness. He urged her on, "Until what?"

"Until I entered some comic book contest my sophomore year in high school." She paused and came back with, "I didn't win. I wasn't even a finalist. So I just stopped making them."

Cosmo struggled to think of something that he had lost. He was always either the winner or a runner up in all of the science contests he had entered as a kid. When he was runner-up, he was glad as it gave the other kids a chance to win. But maybe it didn't matter that he had nothing to compare it to. He could say something to make her feel better and maybe to get her into making comics again. And then it came to him, almost as if the spirit of some wise sage came down and planted the words in his head.

"Who cares about external recognition? You shouldn't. It's fleeting and undependable. All that matters is that you had a good time making those comics. And I think you should start making them again."

Emily reached across the table and put her hand on top of his. "Thank you, Cosmo. That might be one of the greatest things anyone's ever told me. Really!"

"Well, I meant it," he said, noticing how warm and soft her hand felt. "I'd like to see some of those comics too. You didn't throw any of them out, did you?" She shook her head no.

Silvia came to the table just in time to see Emily's hand on top of Cosmo's. She looked down at their hands together with an expression of combined shock and delight, her eyebrows raised and her lips curved in a smile.

"Hope I'm not interrupting anything," she said, sitting down as if she didn't care if she was interrupting them. Emily took her hand off Cosmo's hand, acting natural and unaffected by Silvia's re-entrance.

"Oh, you weren't, Silv," Emily said, turning toward her. "We were just talking about comics."

"Cool," Silvia said, looking down at the nachos as if disappointed that they weren't something else.

"Are you hungry, Silvia?" Cosmo asked, knowing that she didn't want any of the nachos. "We can get something else if you want." Silvia looked back at him, appreciative.

"I want a big cookie, like the one we had in Berkeley," Silvia said, her eyes as young and innocent as a child's eyes.

"I know just the place," Emily said, twirling her hand in the air as if she was doing a magic trick. "There's a café just around the corner, and they have delicious, big cookies." She took some more chips and said to Cosmo, "Let's finish these and split." He liked that she was concerned with finishing the nachos, and that she wasn't one of those overly refined ladies who liked leaving food on her plate. He also liked that she used the dated word 'split.'

As they got ready to leave, it dawned on Cosmo that he had not played any games. How could he have forgotten something like that? "Hey, do you guys mind if I play something before we go?" Usually he wouldn't have asked such a question, but he didn't want to give Emily a bad impression of himself.

"What do you want to play?" Emily asked. "I know where everything is in this place." Cosmo felt like he'd be in love with her before the night was done.

"Alien Storm?" he said to her.

"It's right in that corner," she said, pointing at one of the corners of the bar.

"Thanks," Cosmo said, getting up and heading over to the corner. "I'll be back in a few." He figured it would be good to give Emily and Silvia some time alone, and felt that he also needed some time alone after this rollercoaster of a day.

As he played on the machine, he felt like he was re-living his boyhood days in the arcades on the boardwalks and in the malls. He preferred the boardwalk arcades to the ones in the malls, but in the wintertime, he had no choice because his family never went to the shore in the winter. Even if they did go in the winter, there was a scant chance that any of the arcades would be open. He felt as if he could almost smell the salty sea air combined with the smells of pizza and caramel popcorn. He could almost see Donna coming into the arcade with

Vince, Silvia, and Angie to tell him that his time was up. A part of him longed for this simple time when his biggest concern was having enough time to play in the arcades on the boardwalk.

Chapter 13

When he woke the next morning on the hardwood floor of Emily's apartment, he felt so grateful to the voice inside himself who steered him to finish his journey. He got up and went over to the window, looking outside at the light rain and the trees filled with bright pinkish orange leaves. It was hard to imagine that when he left Philly, the leaves were also fall colored. It felt like another lifetime ago. The storm inside of him that blew and howled only just yesterday had calmed down to the same level of the gentle rain that he watched falling from the pale gray sky outside. The dilemma that was so gigantic had shrunk down to microscopic size, which seemed to be the right size for it.

He looked outside again to see a guy about his age walking down the street, playing with a yo-yo. There sure were some characters here. Maybe he'd have fun living in a place with bars filled with retro arcade machines and adults that played with yo-yos and rode skateboards. Even the living room of Emily's apartment had childlike things scattered around it, including stuffed animals, the board game Monopoly, and a hula-hoop. She also had many adult things though, such as bookshelves crammed with literary classics. It was a humble, small place, but had a feeling of openness to it, which Cosmo attributed to the high ceilings and the fact that it was neat, clean, and uncluttered. He imagined that Emily kept up on her cleaning.

Just as the thought of her came into his head, he heard the door to her bedroom open, and she came out dressed in sleep clothes and messy hair that was almost as wild and all over the place as his own. Still, her face shimmered through her mess of a head of hair, and her prettiness came through even in her sloppy t-shirt and worn down sweatpants. A small, black cat followed her out of the bedroom, as if there was an invisible string that attached them together.

"Hey guys," Emily said, looking over at the couch to see that Silvia was still sleeping. "Oops," she said quietly, putting her hand over her mouth and opening her eyes wide. "I didn't know she was still sleeping."

"Yeah," Cosmo said, smiling. "She loves to sleep, and she can usually sleep through anything."

"Lucky thing," Emily said. She then turned to Cosmo and said, "Hungry? I got cereal, toast, and fruit."

"Oh no, Emily. Let us take you out for breakfast. I insist."

"Oh, thank you," Emily said, looking delighted at Cosmo's suggestion. "We should wait until she wakes up to go out. I'll make us some coffee while she's sleeping."

"Sure. Sounds good," Cosmo said, wondering if Emily wanted to spend some time alone before all going for breakfast. As they walked into the kitchen, he said, "Cute cat. What's its name?"

"Lulu," Emily said, picking up the cat, who curled up in her arm like there was no place else she'd rather be.

"Like your comic book character," Cosmo said, patting its little head. The cat seemed to like his pets, as she moved her little head toward Cosmo's hand, indicating she wanted more.

"Oh no. You got yourself a full time job now."

"Well, that's good. I could use one," Cosmo said, leaning against the wall in the kitchen, for there was only one chair and it looked uncomfortable and partially broken.

"Speaking of your job, when do you have to be back at it?" Emily said as she put a kettle of hot water on the stove and rinsed out a glass French press carafe. If someone had asked him the same question yesterday, he would have felt strangled by anxiety. But now, he wasn't so shaken or even budged by it. For a second, he wondered if some kind spirit had come to him in his sleep and transformed the anxiety within him to calm.

"Well," he said, stretching his arms up in the air. "It's kind of complicated. I got laid-off, and I heard from a friend that the layoff is over, so I think it's pretty open."

"So you can go back whenever?" Emily said, who looked as if she didn't completely understand what he was saying.

"Kind of," Cosmo said. He was starting to think that it might be easier just to tell her what was really up with him. "I just don't feel like going back is all."

"Are you sick of Philly?" she asked him. "Or your job?"

"A little of both. But more than that, I got into such a rut back there, and I don't want to get into it again."

"I get it," she said nodding.

"You do?"

"Yeah. I was in a rut in Tucson too. I felt stale and tired all the time."

"Yeah," Cosmo said, excited at her being able to relate so closely to this feeling. He opened his eyes wide and said. "I hate that feeling. It stinks."

"Well, since you don't have to go back right away, maybe you can take a couple of weeks and stay here. Silvia's going to be my roommate, so we'll be sharing rent."

"Wow, Emily," he said looking up at her as she poured coffee beans in a grinder. "That's so generous of you. And hey, I'm more than happy to help out with money." He wondered if she made the offer, in part, because she wanted him to stay. Emily waved her hand in the air and said, "Ah, don't worry about it." She then turned the coffee grinder on and said in a louder voice, "Unless of course you want to buy some groceries. That'd be cool."

"I'd love to!" he shouted over the grinder. "Let's go shopping after breakfast!"

Silvia appeared in the entranceway of the kitchen, probably awakened from the combination of grinding coffee beans and shouting. She went right over to Lulu and patted her on the head. "I'm so happy you have a cat, Em. I love cats! They're like my favorite animal. Can I pick her up?"

"Yeah, sure," Emily said. "She doesn't bite."

Silvia picked Lulu up as Emily got out some coffee cups and a container of milk.

"I think we'll make good roommates," Silvia said to Emily.

"Agreed," Emily said.

Cosmo was so glad that Silvia would be living in such a nice situation. He only hoped that she'd find a job soon. She was the most resourceful and adaptable person he knew though, and he was sure that she'd have something in no time. She had told him that she usually had something within a week of moving to a new place. He looked at her cuddling Lulu. He couldn't remember the last time he saw her looking so happy. He wondered if he should tell her about Emily's invitation, but his wondering had ceased once Emily herself mentioned it.

"I told Cosmo he could stay here for a while since he said he doesn't have to rush back to work," Emily said, sitting down at the table and pouring some coffee for herself.

Silvia looked at Cosmo with a huge smile and slight shock in her eyes. "Wow, that's awesome, Cosmo!"

"Well, it's such a kind offer," he said, looking over at Emily. "Thanks again."

"Sure," Emily said, "And thanks for offering to help with groceries."

"Oh, it's nothing," Cosmo said. "And food out is on me too, so where do you guys want to go for breakfast?"

"I want to go somewhere where they have big pancakes," Silvia said. "Or waffles."

"I know just the place," Emily said. "And it's right near my work, so I can go to work from the restaurant."

"Oh," Silvia said, sounding disappointed. "You have to work?"

"Yeah," Emily said. "I have to work 'til close, but I'm off tomorrow. So maybe we can all do something fun. Maybe the Japanese Zen Garden at Washington Park. It's wonderful."

Cosmo felt as though he were walking into a painting as they approached the Zen Garden. The entranceway was up a tree-lined hill, branches loaded with fall leaves. Yellow, orange, and red leaves so bright they glowed. As soon as they entered the park, a silence filled the open space around them. The only sound he heard was a soft, trickling waterfall. As they approached the waterfall, Cosmo could see it rolling gently into a pond filled with moss-covered rocks and surrounded by exotic trees and plants, branches drooping down. Wooden walk bridges and stone-made paths were scattered throughout.

When Cosmo saw a bonsai tree, he said to Silvia, "Hey, remember that miniature bonsai tree Mom got you when you were a kid?"

"Sure do," Silvia said, looking over at Cosmo. "I was so touched by it that it was hard for me to get mad at her after she got me that tree." Cosmo remembered a talk that he and Silvia had had just a few months ago. She had reminded him of how Frank would take him for violin lessons in an effort to calm his anger toward their dad. She must have gotten this from her bonsai tree experience. He recalled Frank taking him for lessons every Saturday morning. He then saw Frank's sad face—the one that he had when they left him at his house. He had to call him right now.

"You guys mind if I sneak out of the garden for a minute?" Cosmo said, knowing that cell phones were not allowed in the sanctuary. "I have to make a phone call."

"That's fine," Emily said, who seemed a bit confused by his sudden request. Silvia looked more than confused. She looked put out with one hand on her hip, the other in the air, and a cynical expression on her face. He knew that once he told her that he was going to call Frank, her opposition to leaving them would fade. And he was right. He began walking away when he realized he didn't have Frank's number, and he turned around and ran back to ask Silvia for it.

"Hey, Silvia," he said. "Do you have Dad's number?"

"Sure," she said, showing him the number on her phone.

He went out the entrance to the park and dialed Frank's number. Although he had no hesitation in calling him, he did wish that he'd get his voicemail so he could leave a message and get credit for the call without having to talk to his dad. No such luck. Frank answered on the first ring. Cosmo imagined he was lonely, and that that loneliness made him pick up the phone quickly.

"Hey, Dad," he said, reluctance in his voice. "It's Cosmo."

"Hey, Cosmo," he said, voice subdued. "How are you?" He didn't sound shocked to get the call, and Cosmo then remembered that he told Frank that he'd be in touch with him when they left New Jersey. He had so many different personas. Cosmo was getting the subdued, re-served, sane version of Frank, and he felt lucky. He must have had just the perfect amount of alcohol in him.

"I'm good. Silvia's good. How are you doing?" Cosmo hoped that his dad would ramble on about some non-sense the way that he usually did so that he wouldn't have to talk. But Frank only said that he was good and then asked, "How's it out there on the road?" He rarely, if ever, took an interest in anyone's life so the question caught Cosmo off guard, but he also felt flattered. Even if Frank wasn't genuinely interested in his son's life, at least he was faking an interest. He wondered, for a second, if his dad was changing, but he then reminded himself of how quickly and how radically Frank could change. And he realized that he was just catching his dad in one of his rare good moods and that this was a gift, along with the many other gifts he had received from the universe this week. So he took his gift and answered the question: "It's beautiful out here. You should see it some time."

"Oh, yeah," Frank said who sounded disinterested and unconvinced. He was a bad actor. Cosmo could hear his dad's distraction loud and clear on the other end of the phone. And as he thought about what to say next, Frank blurted out, "You think you might stay out there?" He actually sounded worried. Again, Cosmo felt caught off guard, and didn't know quite how to respond. Maybe his dad didn't dislike him as much as he thought he did. Or maybe he was just feeling lonely and didn't want to lose another child to the west coast. For the second time in his life, Cosmo felt a need to be sensitive to his dad's feelings.

"I might just stay for a little while until Silvia gets her feet on the ground." Surely Frank would appreciate his son being a good big brother to his daughter.

"That'll be longer than a little while, knowing your sister." They shared a laugh. Cosmo couldn't remember when, if ever, that happened. He knew that this was probably as good as it would ever get, so he enjoyed it as much as he could.

"Well, hey, Dad, it was great talking to you."

"You too, Cosmo. And hey, don't be such a stranger. You should call your father more."

"Yeah," Cosmo said. "Take it easy, and I'll talk to you soon."

Cosmo started walking back into the park when his phone rang. It was Donna. If it were anyone else, he would have let the call go so that he could get back to the garden, but how could he ignore a call from his mom?

"Hi, Mom," he said, taking the call.

"Oh hi, Cosmo," she said, her voice sad and low. "I'm so happy I caught you."

"Everything all right?"

"No, not really. I'm down in the dumps. You know it's the tenth year anniversary of your Uncle Vincent's death, and I'm just really feeling it this year. Maybe because it's a significant one and maybe because I have the space in my life now to feel things like this." She paused. Cosmo didn't speak. He didn't want to interrupt his mom. He wanted to hear everything she had to say. "Why is it that you don't recognize a person's true greatness until they've gone?" She paused again. "Anyway, I just wanted to reach out to you and tell you I love you. You're so much like your uncle." She started to cry, which was something she rarely did. First Angie. Now Donna. He wondered if he was turning into one of those men that women always cried to and hoped that wasn't the case.

"I love you too, Mom," he said. "And you have to know that your brother is still with you, right? He's a part of you and always will be." Cosmo could hear a cessation of his mom's crying. He could also sense her shock over the phone. It wasn't something that he would have ever said before this point in time.

"Wow, Cosmo, I wasn't expecting that," Donna said. "I think that trip may have done you a lot of good."

"It did," Cosmo said.

As soon as he hung up with Donna, he sent a text to Silvia telling her that he was on his way back and she texted him back, telling him where to meet them. He re-entered the park. Although it was a re-entrance, it felt like a new experience. He noticed a gray stone statue of a pagoda he hadn't seen the first time, and he felt the tranquility of this special place all over again.

He found Silvia sitting near a small waterfall, her eyes closed, and her hands resting on knees, palms facing upwards to the sky.

"Hey," he said as he got nearer to her.

She opened her eyes for a second and said, "I'm trying to find inner peace. Go bother Emily. She's over there." Silvia pointed to an enclosed sitting area. He found Emily sitting on a bench inside the stone enclosure and sat beside her.

"Hey," he said.

"Hey," she said. "You called your dad? How's he doing?"

"Good," Cosmo said. "And then my mom called me right after. It was good to talk to her."

"They must miss you," Emily said cheerfully.

"I think my mom might," Cosmo said. "I've only been gone a week though." Still, it felt like a lifetime, maybe because he had gained a lifetime of knowledge in this past week. Not the kind of knowledge that he could have learned in school or from books, but from all of the teachers he had found along the road—Silvia, Clay, Crazy Ted, Leonard, Rachel, the Truck Stop Angel.

He had gained something inside of himself, something that he could never lose. He knew now that it didn't matter whether he stayed in Portland or went back to Philadelphia. Philadelphia was only a place, and that place had no power over him in terms of who he was or who he would be. Going back wouldn't erase the growth inside. Going back didn't mean going back to his old way of being in the world. Going back wasn't going backward.

He knew now why it was so important that he finished this trip, and that the importance of finishing wasn't so much getting to the other side of the country, but getting to the other side of himself, to that part of him that made his life worth living. The part beyond sight and sound and time. The part of him that could create something or receive joy from learning something new.

The part that could be moved by a song, or a sunset, or by love. The part of him that could fly and rise above this place called Earth. The part that would never die, but would go on and on and on.

ACKNOWLEDGEMENTS

Catherine Welch
Ruth & Larry Amernick
The Lit Room Book Literature & Film Reviews
Electric Reads UK
Fantastic Books UK
Yvonne Gill of *Fiction Book Reviews*
Kathleen Higgins-Andersen of *Jersey Girl Book Reviews*
Diane Donovan
Alicia Young
Jodi Hanson of *Chapters & Chats Book Reviews*
Cynthia Shepp Book Reviews
Agnes Ntambi of *Her Book List Reviews*
Book Lovers Attic
Carolyn Paul Branch
Denise Gault
Lisa Binion of *Bella Online Reviews*
Annamae Jacobs
Lydia Brown
William Faure
Heather Fabbian
Connie Porciuncula
Charlotte Sanders
Linda Watson
Robin Levin
Chip Capelli